Also by ROBERT NATHAN

Novels

ONE MORE SPRING

JONAH

ROAD OF AGES

THE ENCHANTED VOYAGE

WINTER IN APRIL

JOURNEY OF TAPIOLA

An Omnibus

THE BARLY FIELDS

— containing these novels

THE FIDDLER IN BARLY

THE WOODCUTTER'S HOUSE

THE BISHOP'S WIFE

THE ORCHID

THERE IS ANOTHER HEAVEN

Selected Poems

THESE ARE BORZOI BOOKS, PUBLISHED BY

Alfred A. Knopf

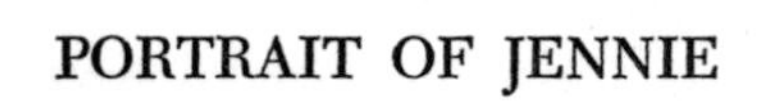

PORTRAIT OF JENNIE

PORTRAIT OF

JENNIE

BY

ROBERT NATHAN

NEW YORK
ALFRED A. KNOPF
1940

FIRST EDITION

MANUFACTURED IN THE UNITED STATES OF AMERICA

Published simultaneously in Canada by
The Ryerson Press

The characters and situations in this work are wholly fictional and imaginary, and do not portray and are not intended to portray any actual persons or parties. (This statement obviously does not apply to those established artists whose names or works are mentioned in this book, or to those families of Truro whom I have also mentioned.)

PORTRAIT OF JENNIE

CHAPTER 1

There is such a thing as hunger for more than food, and that was the hunger I fed on. I was poor, my work unknown; often without meals; cold, too, in winter in my little studio on the West Side. But that was the least of it.

When I talk about trouble, I am not talking about cold and hunger. There is another kind of suffering for the artist which is worse than anything a winter, or poverty, can do; it is more like a winter of the mind, in which the life of his genius, the living sap of his work, seems frozen and motionless, caught — perhaps forever — in a season of death; and who knows if spring will ever come again to set it free?

It was not only that I could not sell my work — that has happened to good men, even to great men, before — but that I couldn't seem to get through, myself, to the things that were bottled up inside me. No matter what I did, figure, landscape, still-life, it all seemed different from what I meant — from what I knew, as surely as my name was Eben Adams, was the thing I really wanted to say in the world; to tell people about, somehow, through my painting.

I cannot tell you what that period was like; because the worst part of it was an anxiety it is very hard to describe. I suppose most artists go through something of the sort; sooner or later it is no longer enough for them just to live — to paint, and have enough, or nearly enough, to eat. Sooner or later God asks His question: are you for me, or against me? And the artist must have some answer, or feel his heart break for what he cannot say.

One evening in the winter of 1938 I was walking home through the Park. I was a good deal younger then; I carried a portfolio of drawings under my arm, and I walked slowly because I was tired. The damp mist of the winter evening drifted around me; it drifted down across the sheep meadow, and through the Mall which was empty and quiet at that hour. The children who usually played there had gone home, leaving the bare, dark trees and the long rows of benches wet and spidery with mist. I kept shifting the portfolio from one arm to the other; it was heavy and clumsy, but I had no money to ride.

I had been trying all day to sell some of my pictures. There is a sort of desperation which takes hold of a man after a while, a dreadful feeling of the world's indifference, not only to his hunger or his pain, but to the very life which is in him. Each day the courage with which I started out was a little less; by now it had all run out, like sand from a glass.

That night I was at the bottom, without money or friends, cold, hungry, and tired, without hope, not knowing where to turn. I think I was a little lightheaded, from not having had enough to eat. I crossed the Drive, and started down the long, deserted corridor of the Mall.

In front of me, the spaced, even rows of lights shone yellow in the shadowy air; I heard the crisp sound of my own footsteps on the pavement; and behind me the hiss and whisper of traffic turned homeward at the end of day. The city sounds were muted and far away, they seemed to come from another time, from somewhere in the past, like the sound of summer, like bees in a meadow long ago.

I walked on, as though through the quiet arches of a dream. My body seemed light, without weight, made up of evening air.

The little girl playing by herself in the middle of the Mall made no sound either. She was playing hopscotch; she went up in the air with her legs apart, and came down again as silent as dandelion seed.

I stopped and watched her, for I was surprised to see her there, all alone. No other little children were in sight, only the mist and the long, even rows of lights stretching away to the terrace and the lake. I looked around for her nurse, but the benches were empty. "It's getting pretty dark," I said. "Oughtn't you to go home?"

I don't believe it sounded unfriendly. The child marked her next jump, and got ready; but first she looked at me sideways over her shoulder. "Is it late?" she asked. "I don't know time very well."

"Yes," I said; "it's late."

“ Well,” she said, “ I don’t have to go home yet.” And she added in a matter of fact tone,

“ Nobody’s ready for me.”

I turned away; after all, I thought, what business is it of mine? She straightened up, and pushed the dark hair back from her face, under the brim of her bonnet. Her arms were thin, they made the sharp, bird-like motions of a child. “ I’ll walk a ways with you, if you don’t mind,” she said. “ I guess it’s a little lonesome here all by myself.”

I said I didn’t mind, and we went up the Mall together, between the empty benches. I kept looking around for someone she might belong to, but there was nobody. “ Are you all alone? ” I asked after a while. “ Isn’t anybody with you? ”

She came to some chalk marks left there by another child, and stopped to jump over them. “ No,” she said. “ Who would there be?

“ Anyway,” she added a moment later, “ you’re with me.”

And for some reason that seemed to her quite enough. She wanted to know what I had in the portfolio. When I told her, she nodded her head in a satisfied way. "I knew they were pictures," she said. I asked her how she knew.

"Oh, I just knew," she said.

The damp mist drifted along beside us, cold, with the smell of winter in it. It was my not having eaten all day that made everything seem so queer, I thought, walking up the Mall with a little girl no higher than my elbow. I wondered if I could be arrested for what I was doing; I don't even know her name, I thought, in case they ask me.

She said nothing for a while; she seemed to be counting the benches. But she must have known what I was thinking, for as we passed the fifth bench, she told me her name without my asking. "It's Jennie," she said; "just so's you'll know."

"Jennie," I repeated, a little stupidly. "Jennie what?"

"Jennie Appleton," she said. She went on to say that she lived with her parents in a hotel, but that she didn't see them very often. "Father and mother are actors and actresses," she declared. "They're at the Hammerstein Music Hall. They do juggling on a rope."

She gave a sort of skip; and then she came over to me, and put her hand in mine. "They're not home very much," she said; "on account of being in the profession."

But something had begun to worry me. Wait a minute, I said to myself, there's something wrong here. Wait, I thought . . . wait a minute . . . and then I remembered. Of course — that was it: the Hammerstein Music Hall had been torn down years ago, when I was a boy.

"Well," I said; "well . . ."

Her hand in mine was real enough, firm and warm; she wasn't a ghost, and I wasn't dreaming. "I go to school," she said, "but only in the mornings. I'm too little to go all day yet."

I heard her give a child's sigh, full of a child's trouble, light as air. "I don't have very exciting lessons," she remarked. "They're mostly two and two is four, and things like that. When I'm bigger, I'm going to learn geography and history, and about the Kaiser. He's the King of Germany."

"He was," I said gravely. "But that was long ago."

"I think you're wrong," said Jennie. She walked a little away from me, smiling to herself about something. "Cecily Jones is in my class," she said. "I can fight her. I'm stronger than she is, and I can fight her good.

"She's just a little girl."

She gave a skip. "It's fun having somebody to play with," she said.

I looked down at her: a child dressed in old fashioned clothes, a coat and gaiters and a bonnet. Who was it painted children like that? Henri?

Brush? One of the old fellows. . . . There was a picture in the Museum, somebody's daughter, it hung over the stairs as you went up. But children always dressed the same. She didn't look to me as though she played with other children very often.

I said yes, I supposed it was fun.

"Don't you have anyone to play with?" she asked.

"No," I said.

I had an idea that she was sorry for me, and at the same time glad that I had nobody else but her to play with. It made me smile; a child's games are so real, I thought, for children believe everything. We came to an interesting crack, and she hopped along on one foot until she got to the end of it. "I know a song," she said. "Would you like to hear it?"

And without waiting for me to answer, looking up at me from under the brim of her bonnet, she sang in a clear, tuneless voice:

Where I come from
Nobody knows;
And where I'm going
Everything goes.
The wind blows,
The sea flows —
And nobody knows.

The song caught me off my guard, it was so unlike what I had expected. I don't know what I had been waiting for — some nursery rhyme, perhaps, or a popular tune of the day; little girls whose parents were actors and actresses sometimes sang about love. "Who taught you that?" I asked in surprise.

But she only shook her head, and stood there looking at me. "Nobody taught me," she said. "It's just a song."

We had come to the great circle at the end of the Mall, and my path led away to the left, across the drive again, and out the west gate. The winter evening wrapped us round in mist, in solitude and silence, the wet trees stood up dark and bare around us, and the distant city sounded its notes, falling and fading in the air. "Well, goodbye," I said; "I have to go now."

I held out my hand to her, and she took it gravely. "Do you know the game I like to play best?" she asked. "No," I said.

"It's a wishing game."

I asked her what she wished for most.

"I wish you'd wait for me to grow up," she said. "But you won't, I guess."

A moment later she had turned and was walking quietly back down the Mall. I stood there looking after her; after a while I couldn't see her any more.

When I got home I heated a can of soup on the gas burner, and cut myself a slice of bread, and some cheese. It was heavy in my stomach, but it made me feel better. Then I took my paintings out of the portfolio, and set them up on the floor, against the wall, and looked at them. They were all New England scenes: Cape Cod, churches, boats, old houses . . . water colors, mostly, with a few drawings among them. But none of the city . . . funny that I had never thought of that before . . .

I went over to the window, and looked out. There wasn't much to see, a line of roofs and chimneys, dark and indistinct, a few lighted windows, and in the north some taller buildings dim against the sky. And over all, the damp, cold air of winter, the raw, heavy air of the coast. A tug boat hooted in the bay; the sad, mysterious sound passed over the roofs, and floated above the city's restless grumble like a sea bird over a river. I wondered why I had never wanted to do any pictures of the city . . . I could do some pastels of the river, I thought, if I could get the cold tone of the sky. And that line of buildings south of the park, in the evening — if I could get that dim blue mountain look they have. But all the time, in the back of my mind, I was thinking about the child I had met in the Mall. Where I am going, nobody knows; The wind blows, And nobody knows. It was a strange little song, its very tunelessness made it hard to forget, the tunelessness was so much a part of it.

I thought of the last thing she had said to me, before she turned and walked away. But people couldn't wait for other people to grow up; they grew up together, side by side, and pace by pace, one as much as the other; they were children together, and old folks together; and they went off together into that something that was waiting — sleep, or heaven, I didn't know which.

I shivered; the big gray dusty radiator in front of the window was only luke-warm. I should have to talk to Mrs. Jekes again, I thought. But I felt suddenly sad, as though someone had just told me an old story about grief. There was no use trying to work any more that night; I went to bed, to keep my courage up.

CHAPTER 2

I WAS behind in my rent again. I think Mrs. Jekes would have asked me to leave, if she could have found anyone to take my place; but nobody wanted a studio like mine, with the furniture falling to pieces, and the ceiling dusty with age. Just the same, she took what I had to say about the heat in very bad part. " This isn't a hotel," she said. " Not for what you pay, it isn't.

"That is," she added grimly, "when you pay it."

I used to dread my meetings with her. She would stand there in front of me, her mouth tight, her thin hands folded across her stomach, and a look in her eyes as though she were seeing through me into the future, and finding it as hopeless as the past. You may wonder that I didn't leave and go somewhere else; but the truth is, I had nowhere else to go. Cheap studios were hard to find; and besides, I was almost always in arrears, and so much without hope myself, those days, that I stayed on because I didn't believe that anything else would be any better.

It was a time of depression everywhere. Hatreds clashed and fought in the air above our heads, like the heavenly battles of angels and demons in the dawn of creation. What a world for a painter; a world for a Blake, or a Goya. But not for me. I was neither — neither mystic nor revolutionary;

there was too much of my mid-western father in me for the one, and too much of my New England grandmother for the other. Yet their heaven had been bright with faith.

I believe that Mrs. Jekes admired my paintings, although she never said so. She used to stand and look at them, with her tight mouth and folded hands; and once she accepted a sketch of the town landing on the Pamet River in Truro, in place of a week's rent. It would fetch a much bigger price today, I suppose, but I doubt if she knows it. Nor do I know what she saw in it — some memory, perhaps, of sunnier days. I had tried to put the stillness of summer into it, the peace of the ever-moving river, the quiet of old boats deserted in the grass. Perhaps she saw it there, too — or only guessed; I don't know.

She didn't care for my pictures of the city. Now that I look back at it, I can see that they were only an old story to her — only the city, in which she was caught like a fly in molasses. What did she care for the cold sky above the river, or the mountain blue of the windy, shadowy streets? She knew them only too well; she had to live her life with them.

But I was full of hope; it lasted for three days. By the end of that time, I had found out that I could not sell my city sketches, either.

It was late in the afternoon of the fourth day that the turn came. I didn't think of it then as a turn; it seemed to me just a piece of luck, and no more.

I was on my way home from tramping about the streets, my drawings under my arm, when I found myself in front of the Mathews Gallery. I had never been there before; it was a small gallery in those days, on one of the side streets off Sixth Avenue. There was a show going on, of some young painter's work — mostly figures and flower pieces; and I went in more or less out of curiosity.

I was looking around when Mr. Mathews came up to me, and asked me what I wanted.

I know Henry Mathews very well by now, I know all about him. In fact, it was he who sold my *Girl In A Black Dress* to the Metropolitan six years ago. I know him to be both timid and kind; he must have hated to see me come in, for he knew at once that I wasn't there to buy anything. But it was getting late, and he wanted to close up; and so he had to get rid of me. Miss Spinney ran the office for him in those days, too; she had gone home, otherwise he would have sent her out to talk to me. She knew how to deal with people who wanted to sell him something.

He came out of his little office at the rear of the gallery, and smiled at me uncertainly. "Yes sir," he said; "what can I do for you?"

I looked at him, and I looked down at the portfolio under my arm. Oh well, I thought, what's the difference? "I don't know," I said; "you could buy one of my pictures, perhaps."

Mr. Mathews coughed gently behind his hand. "Landscapes?" he asked.

"Yes," I said; "mostly."

Mr. Mathews coughed again; I know that he wanted to say to me, My dear young man, there's not a chance. But he could not bring himself to say it; for he dreaded the look in people's eyes when he had to say No. If only Miss Spinney had not gone home — she would have sent me about my business in short order.

"Well," he said doubtfully, "I don't know. Of course, we buy very little . . . almost nothing . . . and the times being what they are . . . However, let me see what you have. Landscapes. Hmm . . . yes; too bad."

I undid the strings of my portfolio, and propped it up on a table. I had no hope of anything, but even to be allowed to show my work, was something. It was warm in the gallery, and I was cold and tired. “Those are some studies from down on Cape Cod,” I told him. “That one is the fisheries at North Truro. That’s Cornhill. That’s the church at Mashpee.”

“Landscapes,” said Mr. Mathews sadly.

All the tiredness, the hunger, the cold, the long waiting and disappointment, caught me by the throat, and for a moment I couldn’t speak. I wanted to take my pictures, and go away. Instead, “Here are one or two sketches of the city,” I said. “There’s the bridge — ”

“What bridge? ”

“The new one,” I said.

Mr. Mathews sighed. “I was afraid of it,” he said.

“And here’s a view from the Park, looking south . . .”

“That’s better,” said Mr. Mathews wanly. He was trying not to look too discouraging; but I could see that he was unhappy. He seemed to be wondering what on earth to say to me. Well, go on, I thought to myself, why don't you say it? Tell me to get out. You don't want any of these . . .

"There's the lake, with ducks feeding . . ."

All of a sudden his eyes lighted up, and he reached out for the portfolio. "Here," he cried; "what's that?"

I looked, myself, with curiosity at the drawing he had in his hand. "Why," I said uncertainly, "that's not anything. That's only a sketch — it's just a little girl I met in the Park. I was trying to remember something . . . I didn't know I'd brought it along with me."

"Ah," said Mr. Mathews happily; "but still — this is different. It's good; it's very good. Do you know why I like it? I can see the past in it. Yes, sir — I've seen that little girl before, somewhere; and yet I couldn't tell you where."

He held it out in front of him; then he put it down, walked away, and came back to it again.

He seemed a lot more cheerful; I had an idea that he was glad because he wouldn't have to send me away without buying anything. My heart began to beat, and I felt my hands trembling.

"Yes," he said, "there is something about the child that reminds me of something. Could it be that child of Brush's up at the Museum?"

I drew in my breath sharply; for a moment I felt again the dream-like quality of that misty walk through the Mall with Jennie. "Not that it's a copy," he said hastily, "or even the same child; and the style is very much your own. There's just something in each that reminds me of the other."

He straightened up briskly. "I'll buy it," he said. But all at once his face fell, and I could see that he was wondering what to pay me for it. I knew that it wasn't worth much, just a sketch done with a little wash . . . if he paid me what it was worth, I should hardly have enough for one decent meal. I am sure now, as I look back on it, that he was thinking so too.

"Look here, young man," he said . . . "What's your name?"

I told him.

"Well, then, Mr. Adams, I tell you what I'll do. I'll take the girl — and that park scene — and give you twenty-five dollars for the pair."

My hands were trembling in good earnest now. Twenty-five dollars . . . that was a lot of money to me then. But I didn't want to seem too eager. What trouble we go to, trying to fool people who see right through us anyhow.

"All right," I said; "it's a deal."

Before he went back to his office to get me the money, he took a little pad out of his pocket, and wrote something down on it. I happened to glance at it where he had left it lying open on the table. It must have been the Gallery expense account, for there were two columns of figures, marked Sales and Expenses. Under Sales he had written: 1 small etching, water scene, Marin, 2nd impression, $35; 1 colored print, blue flower piece, Cezanne, $7.50; 1 litho, Le Parc, Sawyer, pear wood frame, $45.

Under Expenses he had written:

lunch, with beer	$ .80
cigar	.10
hat check	.10
bus (both ways)	.20
stamps	.39
Spinney	5.00
flag from man in veteran's hat	.10
2 water colors, Adams	15.00

For a moment my heart sank, for I had thought he had said twenty-five. But before I had time to feel too badly about it, he came out again with the full amount, two tens and a five. I tried to thank him, but he stopped me. " No," he said, " don't thank me; who knows, in the end I may have to thank you."

He gave me a timid smile. "The trouble is," he said, "that nobody paints our times. Nobody paints the age we live in."

I murmured something about Benton, and John Stuart Curry. "No," he said, "we'll never find out what the age is like, by peering in a landscape."

I must have looked startled, for he coughed in a deprecating way. "Let me tell you something, Mr. Adams," he said. "Let me give you some advice. The world is full of landscapes; they come in every day by the dozen. Do me a portrait of the little girl in the Park. I'll buy it; I'll buy them all. Never mind bridges; the world is full of bridges. Do a great portrait, and I'll make you famous."

Clapping me timidly on the shoulder, he ushered me out into the cold winter air, blue with twilight. But I no longer knew whether it was winter or not. Twenty-five dollars . . .

It was not until long after that I found out the truth about that fifteen dollars in the expense account. It was all he thought they were worth, and he was afraid of what Miss Spinney would say in the morning. He meant to make up the difference out of his own pocket.

CHAPTER 3

So swift is the hot heart of youth, that I thought I had already made a success, and wanted all the world to share it with me. That night I had supper at Moore's Alhambra, on Amsterdam Avenue; for all my glory, that was the best I could do for myself. As I came in, Gus Meyer, who owned the taxicab that used to stand at the corner of our street, waved to me from a table. "Hi, Mack," he exclaimed; "park yourself." He called everybody

Mack; it was his way of telling people that they meant nothing to him personally; or else that he liked them.

"Well," he said, after I was seated, "how are you doing?" He had a big plate of pigsknuckles in front of him, and a glass of beer. "The specialty today," he said; "you'd ought to have some."

Fred, the smaller of the two waiters, came over and I gave him my order. "I'm doing all right," I said to Gus. "I just sold two pictures to an art gallery."

His fork stopped half way to his mouth; and he gaped at me. "You mean you got money?" he asked.

He put his fork down, and shook his head in wonder. "I guess you probably had it coming to you," he said. "But don't lose it, now. Put it in a bank, like you read about in the advertisements."

I told him that most of it would have to go to my landlady, and he looked sorry for me. "An artist don't make so much," he remarked, to comfort me. "It's the same as me. You don't get a chance to lay nothing aside."

For a moment or two he gazed with a peaceful look at his plate. "I had six hundred dollars once," he remarked. "But I spent it."

Almost as an afterthought, he added, "I gave some of it to my mother."

And he returned to his eating, with an air of having finished off the matter.

"This is elegant pigsknuckles," he declared.

For a while we ate in silence. When he was finished, he pushed his empty plate away, and taking a wooden toothpick from a glass on the table, leaned back to remember, and to reflect.

"Some day," he said thoughtfully, "there'll be no more pigsknuckles, and no more beer. When that time comes, I don't want to be here, neither."

"I don't want to be here now," I said; "but I am."

"Well," he said, "you can't do nothing about that. Here you are, and here you stay. So what's it all about? I ask myself."

He gave his toothpick a long, careful look. "But I don't answer," he declared. "You're born poor, and you die poor; and if you got anything, they try to take it off you."

I made the obvious answer, that some men though born poor died rich. "Then they got other troubles," said Gus. "I don't envy them. All I want is a new coil for the cab. She stalls on me."

"I want more than that," I said.

"You got the wrong idea," he said. "I had six hundred dollars once, and I spent it."

I reminded him that he had given some of it away to his mother.

"So what?" he said. "A feller's got a mother, he's got to look after her, don't he?"

"I don't know," I said. "I haven't got one."

"I'm sorry, Mack," said Gus. He remained

downcast, and silent. "Maybe you're married," he said presently. I told him no.

"Well, you're young yet," he said. "Some day you'll meet up with the right one, and you'll be all set." He leaned forward, and looked at me earnestly. "You're a nice kid, Mack," he said. "Put your money in a bank, so when you meet up with the right one, you'll be all set."

I didn't want to talk about things like that. "Listen," I said; "I haven't any money. I never have had any. I just go along, and trust to God."

"Sure," he agreed; "sure. But that don't signify. What you want to ask yourself is, what does God think about it?"

It brought me up short, and made me feel a little uncomfortable. "I don't know, Gus," I said. "What do you think He thinks?"

The toothpick was well chewed out by now; he wrapped his legs around the rungs of his chair, and leaned back. "I wish I could tell you, Mack," he said; " I do indeed. Sometimes you'd almost think He don't know we're here at all. And then when it looks worst, you get a break; along comes a fare for Jersey City, or some drunk tips you what's left of a five dollar bill. That don't make you believe in God, but it shows which way the land lies."

" The pillar of fire," I said, " which went before the chosen people."

But Gus shook his head gloomily. " That was the toughest break we ever got," he said. He brought his chair down, and leaned forward across the table. " Listen, Mack," he said, " did you ever ask yourself what for were we chosen? How I see it is, we weren't chosen for no favors. We were chosen because we were tough; and He needed us like that, so we could tell the world about Him. Well, the world don't want to listen; they want it their way. So they kick us around. God don't care; He says, just keep on telling them."

" And Jesus? " I asked.

" He was a Jew, wasn't He? " said Gus. " He told them; and what did it get Him? If you did what Jesus said today, you'd be kicked around so fast you wouldn't know your tail from a hole in the ground."

He sat up and looked at me, a dark look, like one of the old prophets. " That's where we got a tough break," he said; " being chosen."

" Have another beer," I said; " on me."

" Okay," he said. " I don't mind if I do."

Mr. Moore brought over our beer himself. He was a big man, stout and anxious. " How are you, Gus? " he said. " You look fine. Was everything all right? "

" Elegant," said Gus. " Meet my friend. What's your name, Mack? "

Mr. Moore and I shook hands, and he sat down at our table. " Mind if I sit with you for a minute? " he asked. " Not at all," I said.

"Mack here is a artist," said Gus. "A painter. He just made a lot of money."

The proprietor of the Alhambra beamed at me. "Well now," he said, "that's fine. You satisfied with everything?"

I said yes, that everything was fine.

"We got a nice little place here," said Mr. Moore, looking around slowly, as if he were seeing it all for the first time. "We try to have everybody satisfied."

I felt warm and happy; it was good to be with people, to talk about things without thinking all the time, What am I going to do now?

"You're in a good business, Mr. Moore," I said. "But I guess you know it."

He looked at me, suddenly cautious. "Well, now," he declared, "I don't know. We have a lot of trouble in this business, what with the unions and all. And food costs a lot. We don't make out any too good in this business. At night we don't fill half our tables. It's a lunch business mostly."

"You'd ought to brighten up the place," said Gus. "You take my cab; I give the old bus a going over once a week. Make it shine. That attracts the customers; they like things to look good."

"Sure," said Mr. Moore. "Only I can't afford it."

Gus broke his toothpick in half, and reached for another. "Mack here is a painter," he said. "Leave him paint you something."

Mr. Moore looked from Gus to me; he took up a bowl of sugar, and set it down again. "Well, now," he said, "that's an idea." But I could see that he was waiting to hear what I might have to say.

I thought it was a good idea, too, although it surprised me; it wasn't the sort of thing I would have thought of myself. "Of course," said Mr. Moore. "I couldn't pay much."

" All right," said Gus; " you can feed him, can't you? "

" Yes," said Mr. Moore thoughtfully; " I can feed him."

" Well, Mack," said Gus; " there's your meal ticket."

" It's a good idea," I said.

Mr. Moore gave me a sideways look. " Maybe you could paint me a little something over the bar," he said. " Something tasty, like you'd enjoy standing and looking at."

" He means something with dames in it," explained Gus. " You know — sitting in the grass without nothing on."

The restaurant owner moved uncomfortably; and his fat face grew pink. " It ought to be ladies," he said, " on account of people being a little particular."

" A sort of modern Picnic in the Park," I said, nodding my head. " Yes."

He looked more uncomfortable than ever. “It has to be clean,” he said. “Something that wouldn’t get me into trouble.”

I told him that I thought I knew what he wanted, and he looked grateful. “All right,” he said; “go ahead. You can eat here while you’re doing it, and afterwards, if it’s all right, we can come to an agreement.”

It was not a very business-like arrangement, but we shook hands, and he beckoned to the waiter. “Your little dinner was on me,” he said, taking our bill and scribbling across it.

When we got outside, Gus patted me on the shoulder. “You’re in the money now, Mack,” he said. I tried to thank him, but he waved it aside. “Listen,” he said; “I got my own dinner out of it, didn’t I?”

And as he climbed into his cab, he added with a chuckle,

“Keep it clean, Mack.”

I went home thinking what a good world it was. That night I gave Mrs. Jekes the money for two weeks' rent I owed her, and a week's rent in advance. "What's the matter," she inquired; "you been robbing a bank?"

It didn't even spoil things any, to have her say that. "No," I said. "I'm doing some murals."

CHAPTER 4

It was on a Sunday morning that I saw Jennie again. There had been two or three weeks of clear, cold weather, and the big lake in the Park at Seventy-second Street was frozen, and good for skating. I took out my old pair of Lunns, and went over. The ice was crowded with skaters; I sat down on a bench by the shore to put on my skates, and strapped my shoes to my belt. I stepped off the edge in a wide glide, drew up in a turn that made the snow fly, and set off with the sun in my face.

It was one of those days of beautiful weather such as we get in New York in winter, with a blue-white sky, and light, high, white-grey clouds going slowly over from west to east. The city shone in the sun, roof-tops gleamed, and the buildings looked as though they were made of water and air. I struck out in a long stride, taking deep breaths, feeling young and strong, feeling the blood run warm in my veins, and the air cold and fresh on my face. Couples crossed me, going by with linked hands and red cheeks; schoolboys fled past, like schools of minnows, bent over, on racing skates, cutting ice and wind. An old gentleman was doing fancy figures by himself; dressed in brown, with a red woolen scarf, he swung forward, turned, jumped, and circled backward, his skates together in a straight line, knees bent, and arms akimbo, intent and proud. I stopped and watched him for a moment, and then went on again, into the sun. All around me was the quiet flow of skaters moving and gliding, the creaking sound of steel on ice, the cold air, the bright colors.

I found Jennie near the bridge between the two ponds. She was all in black velvet, with a short, wide skirt, and white boots attached to her round, old-fashioned skates. She was doing a figure eight; and none too well, I thought. But she seemed to me to be taller than I had remembered her — older, too; I wasn't even sure that it was she, until she looked up and saw me. "Hello, Mr. Adams," she said.

She coasted over to me, and put out her hands to stop herself. "I didn't know it was you," I told her. "You look older than last time." She smiled, and pressed the toe of one skate down into the ice, to hold herself. "Oh well," she said; "maybe you didn't see me very good."

I don't know how long we stood there, smiling

at each other. In a little while, Jennie put her arm in mine. "Come along," she said. "Let's skate."

We started off together arm in arm; and once again the world around me grew misty and unreal. Skaters flowing like a river around us, the little flash of steel in the sun, the sound of that river moving, forms seen for a moment and then gone — our own quiet and gentle motion — all served to bring back to me a feeling I had had once before . . . that feeling of being in a dream, and yet awake. How strange, I thought. I looked down at the slender figure at my side; there was no question about it, she was taller than I had remembered.

"It seems to me," I said, "that you've grown a lot since I saw you."

"I know," she answered.

And as I said nothing, but only smiled uncertainly, she added seriously, "I'm hurrying."

She seemed as light as a feather beside me, but I could feel her arm in mine as we skated. I could see the wide black ripple of her skirt flare out as we swung along; and I wondered if we looked like something in an old print. "How are your parents?" I asked her. "Are they having a good season?"

"Yes," she answered. "They're in Boston now."

I thought: and they left you here all alone. But I suppose that's better than taking you everywhere with them . . .

"I did a little sketch of you," I told her, "and I sold it. It brought me luck."

"I'm glad," she said. "I wish I could see it."

"I'll do one some day just for you," I said.

She wanted to know more about the sketch I had made. I told her about Mr. Mathews, and the portrait he had asked me to do; and about Gus, and the picture I was painting over Mr. Moore's bar. She wanted to see that, too; but it was the portrait for Mr. Mathews that interested her most. "Who will it be of? " she asked; I thought that her voice sounded almost too casual. " I don't know," I answered. " I haven't found out yet."

She skated along a moment or two without saying anything. Then, " Perhaps . . . ," she said. And all at once, in a breathless rush — " Will you let it be me? "

Of course, I thought . . . who else? I realized suddenly that there was no one else, that there never could be anyone else for the picture that Mr. Mathews wanted. If only she were a little older . . .

" I don't know," I said. " Perhaps."

She gave my arm another squeeze, and made a wild swoop to the right. " Hooray," she cried; " I'm going to have my picture painted.

" Won't Emily be mad."

" Emily? " I asked.

" Emily is my best friend," she explained. " She had her picture painted by Mr. Fromkes, and I said you were going to do mine, and she said she'd never heard of you, and so I slapped her, and we quarreled."

"Well," I said. "But I thought it was Cecily you always fought with."

She looked away suddenly, and I felt her hand tremble on my arm. "Cecily died," she said in a whisper. "She had scarlet fever. Now my best friend is Emily. I thought you'd know."

"How would I know?" I asked.

She stumbled suddenly. "My shoe is untied," she said. "I've got to stop."

We coasted to the bank, and I knelt down to tie her shoe lace. Kneeling there, I looked up at her, the flushed face of the child, framed in its dark hair, the brown eyes tenderly dreaming, lost in some other time, some other where and when . . . I thought: she is playing at being Cinderella, or perhaps Snow White, so proud to have me kneeling in front of her, tieing her shoe lace.

We had come to shore near the little refreshment booth which they build each year for the skaters, and I asked Jennie if she would care to go in and rest, and if she would like a cup of hot chocolate. She came out of her dream with a long sigh; then her whole body began to quiver, and she clapped her hands gleefully. "Oh yes," she cried. "I love hot chocolate."

Sitting at the counter together, while the hot, watery brew steamed under our noses, we talked about the weather and the world. She wanted to hear, all over again, about how I had sold the sketch of her to Mr. Mathews; and I for my part wanted to know how she was getting along in school. "It's all right," she said, but without much enthusiasm. "I'm having French."

"French?" I asked; startled, because the last time she had been just beginning her sums. "Yes," she said. "I can say colors, and I can count to ten. Un, deux, trois, quatre . . .

" I can say the war, in French. C'est la guerre."

I couldn't make out what she was talking about. " The war? " I asked. " What war? "

But she only shook her head. " I don't know," she said. " It's just the war."

But then her eyes grew wide, and she looked at me in fright. " They won't hurt children like me," she asked; " will they? "

" No," I said. " No."

She took a deep breath. " That's good," she said. " I don't like being hurt."

And she dipped her little nose happily into the chocolate again.

I was happy too, sitting there, with the air smelling of ice and damp wool, peppermint, and wet wood and leather; and Jennie next to me, drinking her chocolate. Perhaps there was something strange about it; but just the same, it felt altogether right, as though we belonged just there, where we were, together. Our eyes met in a glance of understanding; we looked at each other and smiled, as though we had both had the same thought.

“This is lots of fun,” she said.

The chocolate was finished at last; we climbed down from our stools, and clumped our way to the door. “Come along,” I said; “we've time for one more round.” She took my arm, going down the steps to the ice. “I hate it to stop,” she said, “because when will we ever have it again?”

We set off together hand in hand, and made a grand tour of the lake; after that it was time for me to be getting back to work at the Alhambra. I said goodbye to her at the bridge between the two ponds, where we had met. But before I left, I wanted to get one thing straight in my mind.

“Jennie,” I said, “tell me — when did Cecily die?”

She looked away; it seemed to me that her eyes grew clouded, and that her small face grew dim.

“Two years ago,” she said.

CHAPTER 5

"SHE has a look," I said, "of not altogether belonging to today."

I was showing Mr. Mathews some sketches I had made of Jennie in her skating costume, little pictures of the child in motion, doing an inner edge, or poised on her toes as though to run — the same sketches, as a matter of fact, which were shown last year at the Corcoran, as part of the Blumenthal collection. Miss Spinney was there, too, looking over his shoulder; it was my first meeting with her. I liked her dry voice, her sharp, frosty eyes, and her rough way of talking; for her part, she liked my sketches. When it came to painting and painters, there was no getting around Miss Spinney; she judged a man by his work, and nothing else; she wanted it, or she didn't want it.

Mr. Mathews held the sketches out at arm's length, with his head tilted back, looking at them down his nose. "This girl looks older to me than the first one," he said. "But I rather like it, on the whole. She was, perhaps, a little young, before . . .

"Yes," he said; "they aren't bad — are they, Spinney?"

"Is that all you can say?" remarked Miss Spinney. "That they aren't bad?"

Mr. Mathews tilted his head a little to one side, like a bird. "The thing I like about them," he said,

" is the way you've managed to catch that look of not belonging — how was it you said? — not altogether belonging to today. There ought to be something timeless about a woman. Not about a man — we've always been more present-minded."

" You can have the present," said Miss Spinney. " And you know what you can do with it."

Mr. Mathews, who was used to Miss Spinney, went right on. " I don't know what the matter is with women today," he said, sighing. " In my opinion, they lack some quality which they used to have — some quality of timelessness which made them seem to belong to all ages at once. Something eternal — you can see it in all the great paintings from Leonardo to Sargent. Did you ever stop to think how much more real and alive those long-dead women seem to us than the men? The men are done for — finished; there's not a one of them, except perhaps some of the Holbeins, that you'd ever expect to see in the world again. But the women — why, you could meet them anywhere. Mona Lisa, or Madame X . . . on the street, anywhere."

He looked at me accusingly. "The portrait of today," he said, as though it were all my fault, "is planted in the present as firmly as a potato."

"Have you seen Tasker's new portrait of Mrs. Potterly?" asked Miss Spinney.

Mr. Mathews coughed grimly behind his hand. "I understand he received three thousand dollars for it," he remarked.

"One thousand five hundred," said Miss Spinney, "and his trip to Florida."

"One cannot make a living at that rate," said Mr. Mathews.

At my hoarse croak, half envy and half derision, Miss Spinney turned to me and laid a warning hand on my arm. "Now, now, Adams," she said; "control yourself.

"You'll be getting that, too, some day."

It seemed fantastic to me then, fifteen hundred dollars for a portrait; I thought that Tasker must be either a genius or a scoundrel. A man changes his mind about such things as he grows older; but it made me feel bold, and — as I look back at it now — probably a little reckless, too.

"All right," I said; "in that case, what do I get for my sketches?"

"Spinney," murmured Mr. Mathews, "you talk too much."

And Miss Spinney replied almost at the same moment,

"They are hardly worth anything at all."

It was a cruel way to take me down, though I dare say I deserved it. I picked up my sketches, and started to put them away.

"My dear young man," began Mr. Mathews unhappily . . .

"Look here . . ."

But I meant to carry it off with a high hand.

"Goodbye," I said; and to Miss Spinney, "I'm very glad to have met you."

She looked at me for a moment with eyes like black frost. I thought she was going to help me to the door, but all at once, to my surprise, her face grew warm and rosy, and she burst out laughing. "I like you, Adams," she said, and fetched me a terrific clip on the back. "You're proud, aren't you?

"Come along — take them out again, and let's have a look at them."

She went over them a lot more carefully than Mr. Mathews had done; for one thing, she seemed less interested in Jennie, and more interested in my drawing. Mr. Mathews watched her in a timid sort of way; he wanted her to like them, because that would help him to feel right about me. He kept drumming with his fingers on the table, and clearing his throat.

"I suppose it could be the clothes," he said,

"that make her look a little older."

I didn't think so, but I didn't know how to say what I thought; I stood there feeling uneasy, feeling my heart beating a little fast, and wondering what Miss Spinney would say. She put the sketches down at last, and gave me a clear, hard look. "All right, Adams," she said; "we'll give you twenty-five dollars for the lot."

I suppose I might have taken it, if I had been able to forget her remark about the sketches not being worth anything. I was still a little angry, and I wanted to stand up to her. I was young; and I didn't know very much about art dealers. "It isn't enough," I said; and I got ready to go.

I thought to myself that I didn't care, that I'd sell them to somebody else. But I did care, and I had no way of hiding it. "Look, Adams," she said; "you're a nice boy, but you don't know the art business. I know you can paint; but we aren't collectors, we don't buy things we like just for the fun of sitting around and looking at them the rest of our lives. If we buy these sketches, we've got to sell them too. We can give you thirty dollars. What do you say?"

"Yes," said Mr. Mathews eagerly; "what do you say, young man?"

I took a deep breath, and said "Fifty dollars."

Miss Spinney turned slowly away; I thought that she was angry, and I thought what a fool I was being. I was stubborn, but I was unhappy; I looked at Mr. Mathews, but he was looking at Miss Spinney, and drumming on the table. I started to say, "All right, take them," but she didn't wait for me. "The hell with it," she said. "Give him the fifty."

Mr. Mathews jumped with relief. "That's right, Spinney," he exclaimed. "That's right; I'm glad you see it my way."

She shrugged her shoulders. "I'm just a potato, Henry," she said, "with nothing eternal about me. You'll have to sell them yourself."

"Yes," he said. He took up the sketches, looked at them, put them down, and then picked them up again. "Yes," he said; "yes, of course. I'll sell them — never fret; I'll find a customer for them. Not right away, perhaps . . ."

They gave me fifty. It doesn't seem important now, but it did then. I was getting my meals at Moore's Alhambra, and so it seemed like a fortune to me, almost as much as Tasker's fifteen hundred. I suppose it seemed like such a lot because it was my own. It was real, and I could spend it.

Before I left, Mr. Mathews spoke to me again about doing a portrait for him, but this time he said in so many words that he wanted it to be of Jennie. "There's something in the girl," he declared, "reminds me of something . . . I haven't placed it yet, but I can tell you what it feels like. It feels like when I was young."

He looked up at me apologetically. "I don't know if I can express it any other way," he said. "I shouldn't think you'd understand."

But I thought I understood. "Do you mean that she's old fashioned?" I asked.

"No," he said, "that isn't what I mean. Not altogether."

"Well, I do," I replied. "I think she's old fashioned."

Miss Spinney saw me to the door. "Goodbye," she said; "come in again. And if you have any nice flower-pieces, about two or two and a half by four . . ." She looked around for Mr. Mathews, and seeing him behind her with his back turned, lowered her voice to a whisper. "I like flower-pieces," she said.

I went over to Fifth Avenue, because that was the avenue I wanted to walk on. For the first time I felt that it was my world, my city, that it belonged to me, to my youth and to my hopes; there was a taste of exultation in my mouth, and my heart, filled with joy, lifted like a sail and carried me along with it. The windy, high walls over my head, the wide and gleaming shop windows strung out before me with their mingled colors, the women's bright, hard faces, and the sun over everything — the sun and the wind —

I thought of Jennie's song. And then I thought to myself that I didn't know where she lived, or even how to find her; and the light went out of everything.

CHAPTER 6

" So what you want," said Gus, " is I should find a girl whose name is Jennie. You don't know where she lives, nor nothing about her. So you've got what I would call a good start."

" Her parents are jugglers," I told him. " On a tight rope."

" That makes it easier," he said. " Are they on the circuit? "

I didn't know. I told him that their name was Appleton.

" Appleton," he grumbled; " Appleton." He set himself to think for a moment. " There used to be an act called by that name," he declared. " Down at the old Hammerstein."

" That's right," I said eagerly. " That's where they were."

Gus looked at me strangely. " Well, then, Mack," he said, " they'd be in the old folks' home by now. This must be some other people.

" You sure you seen this girl? "

" Yes," I said. " I made some sketches of her."

He shook his head uncertainly. " That don't signify," he remarked. " I was thinking maybe you made her up."

" No," I said. " I didn't make her up."

We were standing in front of his cab, on the corner, in the grey, raw, morning air. There was snow coming. I could smell it back of the wind, and I shivered a little. But Gus, in his two tattered sweaters, one over the other, didn't seem to feel it; he was used to cold, as he was to heat; he made me think of some old fisherman at Truro, whipped by years of weather, blackened and toughened by the sea. But there was no clear salt for Gus; his tides and channels were the streets, and his face was a city face, pale, quick to anger, quick to rejoice, alert, sly, and confident. None of the slow brooding of the ocean there, the patient, sea-way thought . . .

"I'll take a look around if you want," he said, "and ask some people I know. But listen, Mack —" his voice sank to a low and urgent level — "don't go getting into any trouble with the police. A girl as young as that —

"I don't want no trouble myself, neither," he added as an afterthought.

"All I want to do," I said, "is to paint her picture."

And I thought that was all; I would have sworn that was all I wanted.

Back in my studio again, I tried to work. I was doing a fair-sized canvas of the lake with the skaters on it, from memory and from some sketches, but it was hard to get on with. My heart wasn't in it; my mind flew off in a dozen directions at once. I kept wondering whether I oughtn't to start a flower-piece for Miss Spinney, and whether Gus would be able to find out anything about the Appletons; and I kept thinking about the Alhambra, about my picture over the bar; there was still a lot of work to be done on it. I was restless and uneasy, my brush was uncertain, and the light was poor. I was glad when it was lunch time, and I could put my things away, and go out.

Gus wasn't at the restaurant when I got there. I ate by myself, and then put up my step-ladder back of the bar, and went to work. He came in after I had been working about an hour, and sat down at a table where he could watch me. I looked down at him anxiously, but he shook his head.

"No luck, Mack," he said. "I'm sorry."

"Didn't you find out anything at all?" I asked. He looked back at me with a strange expression on his face. "There were some Appletons did a tight wire act, like I thought," he said, "back in 1914. They had a sort of accident; it seems the wire broke on them one day, back in '22."

We stared at each other for a moment, and then the waiter came with his beer. Gus took a long drink, and, leaning back, gazed solemnly up at my picture. "It's coming along fine," he said.

I had painted a picnic by the shore of a lake not unlike the lake in the Park; and there, by the side of the water, under the trees, my women were gathered to tease and gossip on the grass. They were innocent figures, and I knew that Gus thought that they could do with some men. To that extent he was a realist; but he did not go to extremes. What he asked of a picture was simply this: that it should remind him with the clearest force of what he already knew, along with some further suggestion of a better and a happier world.

"Yes, sir," he declared; "when I see things like that, I think I've been wasting my time."

All at once he sat up in his chair, and pointed to the figure of a young woman lying on her side, her face half turned away, at the edge of the water. "What's the matter with that one?" he demanded. "She don't look so good to me."

"Why?" I asked carelessly, without looking up. "What's the matter with her?"

"She looks drowned," said Gus.

I turned quickly back to the picture. "What do you mean?" I said. But even as I spoke, I saw what he meant; there was something about the way I had placed her under the trees which made her face seem dim, and green with leaf-shadow; her dark hair gave the impression of being wet, and her whole body seemed shadowy with water . . . I felt an indefinable anguish as I looked at it, which I attributed to anger at my own lack of skill; and reached hurriedly for my tube of raw umber.

But even after I had brought her out into the sun again, I felt a depression which I could not account for. It was that figure, half seen, half hidden, which I had imagined secretly in my heart to be Jennie — as she would some day be — and I could not bear to think that brush and heart had so failed each other.

However, Mr. Moore was well satisfied with the picture. "Well, now," he said, coming over and looking up at me where I sat on my stepladder, "that's just about what I wanted. Yes sir, that's what I had in mind. I'd call it entertaining, but it don't offend. I've got a spot over the service door I've been thinking about; we could maybe do a little something there."

"What's the matter," said Gus; "you want a museum?"

"I like to have it nice here," said Mr. Moore. "A picture brightens things up for the customers."

"All right," said Gus; "tell him to do one of me and my cab. That'll be nice for you, and nice for me, too.

"Only make it look good," he added. "Don't drown me."

The first snow was falling as I went home, small flakes coming down slowly, twisting down through the grey levels of air, on the north east wind. The whole city was grey under the heavy sky which seemed to press against me as I walked. I thought of the Cape, of how this storm must be already singing across the dunes, driving its wet snow in from the sea over the little houses huddled in their hollows, the foam breaking below the cliff at High Land, the thunder of surf filling the long nooks and valleys like the sound of trains rolling and rumbling behind the hills — the storm and the snow driving south, out of the black, empty, wrinkled ocean, out of Labrador, out of Greenland waters dark with winter and night. How little we have, I thought, between us and the waiting cold, the mystery, death — a strip of beach, a hill, a few walls of wood or stone, a little fire — and tomorrow's sun, rising and warming us, tomorrow's hope of peace and better weather . . . What if tomorrow vanished in the storm? What if time stood still? And yesterday — if once we lost our way, blundered in the storm — would we find yesterday again ahead of us, where we had thought tomorrow's sun would rise?

I let myself into the house, shaking the snow from my shoulders on the door sill. As I stood there in the hall, which was as cold and somber as myself, Mrs. Jekes came out of her parlor and looked at me with eyes in which there was suspicion, resentment, and a curious excitement. It was apparent that she had been waiting for me. "Well," she said; "there you are. Hah."

And she folded her hands virtuously in front of her.

I looked back at her without speaking. My rent was paid, and I couldn't think of any reason to be anxious. I had an idea that she disliked me, and that she was glad to have some bad news for me; but what she said next, wasn't what I expected at all.

"You have a visitor," she said. "A young lady."

And as I only stared at her with my mouth open, she added harshly,

"Fine doings, I must say."

With a sniff of disdain, she turned to go back into her parlor again. "The young lady is waiting for you upstairs," she said, and closed the door, as though to say "I wash my hands of all of it."

I went up slowly, puzzled and concerned, my heart beating fast. I had no friends, there was no one it could be. It seemed impossible that anyone should be waiting for me.

But I was wrong. I knew it even before I opened my door; some inner sense told me.

It was Jennie. She was sitting in the old chair near the easel, prim and upright, her hands tucked away in a little muff in her lap, her toes just touching the floor, a round fur bonnet like a little cake on the top of her head. I came in slowly, and leaned for a moment against the side of the door, looking at her. I felt almost weak with happiness.

"I thought maybe you wanted me to come, Eben," she said.

CHAPTER 7

SHE sat quietly in the big chair while I put away my brushes and went to look for something with which to make tea. Her gaze, moving slowly about, lingered on everything, the shabby furniture, the dusty walls, the stacked canvases on the floor, the closet bursting with odds and ends of clothing, sketches, paints, cans, and broken boxes, the tumbled cot with its dilapidated blankets — all that I myself had never thought to look at very carefully, or even notice, before she came. But now I saw it all, and for the first time, as she did. Her eyes widened, and she took a long breath.

"I've never been in a studio before," she said. "It's lovely."

The tin kettle still had some water in it left over from the morning, so I lit the gas ring under it, and went to search in the closet for a box of crackers. "It's an awful place, Jennie," I said. "It's pretty dirty."

"Yes," she agreed, "it is. I didn't want to say it . . . but I guess as long as you said it first . . ."

She got up, and took off her bonnet and laid it with her coat and her muff very neatly on the chair. "I don't suppose you have an apron?" she asked. "And something to dust with?"

I looked at her in consternation. "You're not going to try to clean it?" I cried.

"Yes," she said. "While the water's boiling . . ."

All I could find was a towel and a clean handkerchief. She tied the handkerchief over her hair and under her chin, the way they do on the Cape, and took up the towel with an air of determination. Then, with her slender legs planted wide apart, she looked around once more like a general before a battle, and her face fell. "Oh goodness," she cried; "I don't know where to begin."

I found the crackers, and some lumps of sugar for the tea, and I went down the hall to rinse the cups in the basin. I peered over the bannisters as I went by, to see what I could see; sure enough, there was Mrs. Jekes standing very still in the hall below, listening with all her might. I wondered what she expected to hear, and let out a shrill whistle, to show her what I was doing. She looked up, startled, and then scuttled back into her room again.

When I returned to the studio, Jennie was seated on the floor, the dust-rag towel beside her, and my sketches of the city spread out around her. Smiling, she looked up at me as I entered, a dark smudge across her chin, and another along her arm between her wrist and elbow. " I was looking at these," she said. " Do you mind? "

I told her no, of course I didn't mind.

" They're beautiful," she said. " I think you're a very good artist. Only, some of them . . ." she held a small canvas up to the light . . . " I don't know where they are. I've never seen those places."

I glanced over her shoulder as she sat there on the floor. She was looking at a little picture I had done in tempera of the skyscrapers at Radio City. " Yes," I said; " well . . . they're new, I guess. They haven't been built very long."

" I guess that's it," she agreed.

She looked for a long time at the picture, holding it out toward the window, toward the last grey light of afternoon. " It's funny," she said at last, "how sometimes you've never seen things, and still, you know them. As though you were going to see them some time, and because you were going to see them you could remember what they looked like . . . That doesn't sound right, does it?"

"I don't know," I replied. "It sounds pretty mixed up."

"I guess so," she said. "I guess it does. You couldn't remember what you hadn't ever seen."

She sat with the picture on her lap, staring in front of her. It was almost dark by now in the room, the snow outside, falling more heavily, making a grey light in the window, and everything in shadow. She seemed to be gazing through the shadows themselves into some other where, somewhere far off and strange, for her bosom rose and fell, her lips parted, and a long sigh escaped her. The snow, caught in a sudden rift of wind, made a soft, spitting sound on the window pane, and in the river somewhere a boat sounded its lonely hoot.

She stirred uneasily; her hand crept up and touched mine. "No," she said in a whisper; "you couldn't possibly."

I went over and snapped on the lights, and the bare, untidy room sprang out of the gloom at us, harsh and real, its four stained walls holding the present in a cube of unmoving light. Jennie gave a sort of cry, and rose to her feet. "What a silly," she said; "here I haven't dusted hardly at all."

"Never mind," I told her; "the water's boiling. Let's have our tea."

She was all gayety after that, sitting up in the chair again, with her toes barely touching the floor, pouring water out of the rusty kettle, passing the crackers, and talking happily about a thousand things. I had to tell her all about Miss Spinney, who had such a hard heart and liked flower-pieces, and how we had fought over the sketches, and I had won; and she clapped her hands with excitement. "Oh Eben," she cried, "you are a good one." She wanted to hear about Gus and his taxicab; she thought he must be very rich to have a cab of his own. "Do you think some time he'd let me ride in it?" she asked. "I've never ridden in a taxicab.

"But I've been in a hansom, once, with mother in the Park; the driver sat up on top, and had a high hat."

She told me that her friend Emily was going away to boarding school. "I think perhaps I'll go with her," she said. "It's a convent, really, called St. Mary's, but it isn't Catholic. It's on a hill, and you see the river; and Emily says they go out every Easter and bless the pigs. I don't want to go very much, but mother says I have to, and anyway, Emily's going . . . I'll miss you, Eben."

"I'll miss you, too, Jennie," I said. "Will you pose for me, before you go?"

"I was hoping you'd say that," she answered. "Yes, I will."

" Will you come tomorrow, then? "

But she looked away, and her face took on a puzzled expression. " I don't know," she said. " I don't know if I can."

" The day after? "

She shook her head. " I'll come as soon as I can," she answered; and that was all she would say.

I told her about Tasker's portrait of Mrs. Potterly, and the great price — as it seemed to me — he had got for it. Her face lit up, and she gave a little laugh. " Will you be glad to be so rich? " she asked. " You mustn't forget me."

" Forget you? " I cried incredulously.

" Oh well," she said; " when you're rich and famous.

" But I guess you won't," she added contentedly. " Because maybe I'll be rich and famous too, and we can be it together."

I said: " I don't think I care very much about

being rich, Jennie. I just want to paint — and to know what I'm painting. That's what's so hard — to know what you're painting; to reach to something beyond these little, bitter times. . . ."

"Are these bitter times, Eben?" she asked in surprise.

I stared at her, thinking: of course, how would she know about bitterness, how would she know about the artist at all? caught in a mystery for which he must find some answer, both for himself and for his fellow men, a mystery of good and evil, of blossom and rot — the mystery of a world which learns too late, always too late, which is the mold, and which the bloom . . .

She had been watching my face, and now she held out the box of crackers to me. "Here," she said, "take one. Then you won't feel so bad." I burst out laughing at myself, at both of us; and she laughed, too.

But presently she grew serious again. "You're

not sad any more, are you, Eben? " she asked. " I mean — you were so sad the first time I saw you."

" No," I said, " I'm fine now. I was scared that night I met you. I felt as though I were lost. . . ."

She cowered down in her chair, and put her hands up as though I were about to strike her. " No," she cried out, " Oh no — don't ever say that, not ever again. And besides, you weren't lost — you were here, and here isn't lost. It can't be; it mustn't be. I couldn't bear it."

And turning to me almost piteously, she added, " We can't both of us be lost."

It lasted only a moment, and then it was gone — and we were back again, in my room, with the yellow-lighted walls, and the grey snow outside, and my pictures spread out on the floor about me, the world I knew, the world I saw every day real and around me. " No," I said, " I'm not lost. Why should I be?

“What a foolish way to talk.”

She smiled up at me in a forlorn sort of way. “Yes,” she said; “it's foolish. Don't let's talk like that any more.”

“Because,” I said, “with little girls like you . . .”

“Yes,” she agreed gravely; “little girls like me.” She got up, and gave me her cup, and the tea pot. “Here,” she said. “You go and wash them out, before you forget.”

“All right,” I said. “Wait for me; I'll be right back.”

“Yes,” she said. “I'll wait for you.”

I went down the hall; it was dark on the stairs; the door of Mrs. Jekes' parlor was tight shut. I could hear the snow pitting down on the skylight in the roof. I rinsed the cups out, and hurried back. “Jennie,” I said.

But she was gone; and the room was empty.

I hadn't heard her go; I hadn't heard the hall door close. But she was gone.

It wasn't until later that I remembered that I hadn't even asked her where she lived.

CHAPTER 8

After the storm, the city sparkled for a little while; then the snow was gone, upgathered in hard white hills and carted off in trucks to the river. For a day the air was full of winter sounds, the sounds a child remembers from his youth — the wooden tock of shovels on the ice, the clink of picks, the whine and whirr of motors, and the little musical note of chains over the snow. I did a sketch of the river, with its swift and leaden current, and a little oil painting of the Park, with children coasting. But mostly I was content to do nothing, to wander in the city, and to let my mind drift where it pleased. I kept thinking about the portrait I wanted to do of Jennie, and wondering when I would see her again. I no longer thought of her as a child. She seemed to me at that time to be of no particular age, or at that age between ages when it is impossible to say that the child is a young lady, or that the young lady is still a child. From the mystery which surrounded her, my mind hung back, my thoughts turned themselves away. It was enough for me to believe that wherever in this world she actually belonged, in some way, for some reason, she belonged with me.

Even if I had known, it could have made no difference; I can see that now. It was not in my hands, nothing was in my hands; I could not bring the spring nearer before its time, I could not keep the winter from vanishing behind me.

Sometimes in late summer or in early fall there is a day lovelier than all the others, a day of such pure weather that the heart is entranced, lost in a sort of dream, caught in an enchantment beyond time and change. Earth, sky, and sea are in their deepest colors, still, windless, and shining; the eye travels like a bird out across the distance, over the motionless air. All is fixed and clear, never to end, never to change. But in the evening the mist rises; and from the sea comes the grey warning.

In Truro they call it a weather breeder. So it was with me; it seemed to me that the entire world was bathed in a pure and peaceful light. Death had been arrested, and evil was far away; man's cries, the madness, the anguish, were stilled, and in the stillness, like far off surf, I heard the sound of yet more distant things. For beyond the close horizon of death, there is something else; beyond evil, some spirit untouched, untroubled, and remote.

Once upon a time, not so very long ago, men thought that the earth was flat, and that where earth and heaven met, the world ended. Yet when they finally set sail for that tremendous place, they sailed right through it, and found themselves back again where they had started from. It taught them only that the earth was round.

It might have taught them more.

This short and happy season was made even happier for me, by the visit of my friend Arne Kunstler, from Provincetown. He arrived one morning in his sheepskin jacket, big, red-faced, and bearded like an artist of the 'eighties. But the resemblance stopped with his beard; there was nothing else of the 'eighties about him. He brought a bundle of canvases down with him from the Cape, and set them up on stretchers in my room. The wild and violent pictures flamed at me from the walls and from the floor, like scenes from an inferno. Next to them, my own paintings seemed restrained and mild, colorless and discreet.

He was not pleased with me. "What is this work you are doing, Eben?" he cried. "Portraits — flower-pieces — what has come over you? Not," he added, "that you ever were on the way to being an important painter; but I always thought there was hope for you, at least."

His voice, like that of an old sea-captain, was always pitched at half a gale. Poor Arne, I never took him very seriously, for all his roaring; and as for his painting, I had long ago given up trying to understand it. But I was fond of him, for we had been students together; and I was delighted to see him. His mind was a cave of winds, blowing from all corners at once, a tempest of ideas; he was in love with color, he was like a Viking gone berserk in a rainbow. He lived on next to nothing: I doubt if he sold more than a canvas a year. But he was a happy man, for he never doubted his own genius.

His wants were few; and his sorrows were vast, and without pain.

His favorite remark was this: " Art should belong to the masses." But when I declared that the masses would never understand his paintings, he stared at me in astonishment. " Understand? " he thundered; " understand? Who asked them to understand?

" Art can have meaning only to the creative spirit itself.

" Besides," he added, " the masses aren't as stupid as you think. Look how they took to Homer."

" Not to his water colors," I replied. " And anyhow, what in the name of heaven have you and Homer in common? "

He couldn't answer that, of course. " Oh, well," he mumbled, half in his beard, " I was only trying to show you . . . But you'll see," he bellowed, " just the same."

He brought the past back with him, the old, free, careless days in the wind and sun of New England, the winter at the Atelier Dufoix in the Rue St. Jacques — the great cold shadowy room with its charcoal stove, and the shivering students, the evenings in the little bistro on the Boule Miche' — the early lessons here at the Academy, under Hawthorne and Olinsky — days of work, and nights of argument, when it was enough to settle forever such things as the eternal verities, and never stop to think of what was to become of the artist and his pictures. I took him to the Modern, to see the Modiglianis, and to the Ferargil, to see the single Brockhurst, my own favorite; but he was as contemptuous of the one as of the other, he had no use for any work except his own.

It was the city he admired most, and coming from the flat, windy winter on the Cape, he helped me to see with fresh eyes the soaring stone, the sun-drenched skylines, the brawling shadows all around me. And my heart, in which the old brew of doubt and anxiety had already begun to clear, stirred by hope, by the bright weather, and by something else which I did not know how to name, opened itself in a thrust of joy to the future.

Needless to say, Mrs. Jekes took an instant dislike to him. The very first night, she came hurrying up the stairs, pale and grim, to ask us to make less noise — though she did not so much ask us, as tell us, standing there in the doorway with her hands folded across her stomach, and her eyes steeped in bitterness. "I don't know what sort of a house you think this is," she said, "or what you think you're doing in it; but there's others want to sleep if you don't, and I can always call the police if I have to."

I can hardly blame her, for we were young, and happy, and we must have been making a lot of noise. I was afraid that Arne would throw something at her, but after one long, startled look, he only mumbled, " Yes ma'am," and went off into a corner. After she had left, marching down the stairs with a tread like an army, I saw that he was pale, and actually uneasy. I started to laugh at him, but he stopped me. " No, Eben," he said, " you're wrong to laugh. That's a dreadful woman. She comes in here like black ice, and my pictures freeze over. Oh no, Oh no, I am going to whisper from now on."

But although I laughed at him, I remembered what he said.

For a week or so, I roamed about the city with Arne, delighting in the fine weather, and in the companionship of my friend. I took him to the Alhambra where, I need hardly add, he thundered at my mural like Dufoix himself in the old days in Paris. In his opinion, I had painted a stupid and vulgar scene; nevertheless, with a plate of sauerbraten in front of him, he went so far as to consider the possibility of doing a panel himself, perhaps the one over the service door, in return for a week's good eating. Mr. Moore thought it over for a while, but after he had seen an example of Arne's work, he shook his head regretfully. " It's not that I don't think Mr. Kunstler is a fine artist," he said, " but I've got to think of the customers. I want everybody to be satisfied around here."

" Never mind," said Arne. " Forget it."

" Yes," said Mr. Moore. " Well, thanks for the offer."

It was Gus who did his best to console him. " Never mind, Mack," he said; " some people don't have no eye for anything but their food. Now you take me; I like to look at something pretty when I got the time. But you take most people, they don't feel that way. What they say is, bring in the soup, and get on with it."

" Forget it," said Arne. He waved his arm in a dignified way. " The artist ought not to have to paint for a living," he declared. " Eben, let us all have another glass of beer, and I will repay you some day when I am able."

"Ho," said Gus; "there's a man for you."

His big, red-knuckled hand wrapped around his glass, Arne beamed at us all. "Here's to art," he said.

"And to friends," I added.

"Any friend of Mack's here is a friend of mine," said Gus.

We dipped our noses into the yellow foam. "Just the same," said Arne in a mild bellow, coming up for air, "art can only mean something to the artist who creates it."

CHAPTER 9

ARNE went back to Provincetown by boat and bus, leaving behind him by way of a gift, or to repay me for his bed and board, a picture of what he said was a sunset, all in such tones of light as had never been seen on earth before, at least not since the age of reptiles — and which, once his back was turned, I lost no time in hiding under the bed.

During the fortnight which followed, I was busy both at home and at the Alhambra. Among other things, I finished a flower-piece for Miss Spinney, and took it down to the gallery to give to her. As I had feared, Mr. Mathews groaned when he saw it. "Look here," he exclaimed; "whatever put that into your head? A flower-piece . . . and gladiolas, of all things. What do you expect me to do with it, young man?"

I replied that Miss Spinney had asked for it, and that gladiolas were all that I could get at the florist. "It's winter now," I reminded him. "There aren't any summer flowers."

"Spinney," said Mr. Mathews, "you will be my death."

And he gave a cry of indignation.

"Never mind," said Miss Spinney calmly; "I like it. Give Adams thirty dollars, and I'll sell it myself before the week is up."

But for once Mr. Mathews refused to be bullied.

Faced with a flower-piece, he put his foot down. " Twenty-five," he said, like a mouse at bay, " and not a penny more."

Miss Spinney looked at him carefully; she knew when to insist, and when to give in. " All right," she said; " twenty-five, then. Is that enough, Adams? "

As a matter of fact, I would have let her have it for less than that, or for nothing. " It isn't enough," I said, " but I'll take it."

" You're hard as nails, aren't you? " she said with her wintry smile. " So am I. That's why I like you.

" Just the same," she added grimly, " we've lost money on you so far. So don't go getting ideas."

Mr. Mathews scratched his chin in an unhappy way. " Well now," he said uncomfortably, " that isn't strictly true, Mr. Adams. I mean to say, we've only sold one sketch, but of course we still have the others."

" Forget it," said Miss Spinney. " Adams here is all right. He understands me."

Nevertheless, as I went out, she drew me aside and pressed a five dollar bill into my hand. " When I say thirty," she declared, " I mean thirty." I tried to give it back to her, but she pushed me out of the door. " On your way, Adams," she said; " on your way. Don't irritate me."

The next day I prepared a five foot canvas; I stretched and mounted it, wet one side of it with water, and worked in a light surface of white lead with my palette knife. Then I set it out to dry. It was a trick Jerry Farnsworth had taught me up on the Cape.

After that there was nothing to do but wait.

Jennie came at the end of the week. I heard her light step on the stairs, and ran to open the door. She looked pale, I thought, and she was dressed in some kind of mourning. She stood in the doorway, and looked at me in a pitiable way.

“It’s father and mother,” she said. “They had an accident.” She tried to smile, but her eyes filled, and she had to wink hard to keep the tears back. “They’re dead,” she said, almost in surprise.

“I know,” I answered, without thinking; and then bit my lip. I took her hand, and led her into the room. I thought that I ought to say something, that I ought to explain how I knew . . . “I read about it,” I told her. “In the paper.”

“Oh,” she said vaguely. “Yes.” But she wasn’t thinking about me.

I made her sit down, and took her hat and coat and laid them on the bed. “I’m sorry, Jennie,” I said.

She drew a deep breath. “They were sweet to me,” she said in a voice which trembled a little. “I didn’t use to see them very much. But . . . the way they died . . .”

“I know,” I said.

“Oh Eben,” she cried; and hid her face, and wept.

I wanted to comfort her; but I thought it would be better if I let her cry herself out. Turning my back, I walked over to the window, and stared at the deep blue sky. “Look,” I said after a while; “you don’t want to pose, do you? I mean — after this?”

I wasn’t looking at her, but I could hear her sit up, and blow her nose. “I wanted to come,” she said unevenly. “I wanted to see you. Just to be here.” She gave a little hiccup, after crying; and then a shaky sigh. “I might as well pose,” she concluded. “I don’t look very pretty, though.”

I thought that if anything, she looked prettier than before. The tears had left no mark on her young face, but they had washed her eyes and left them dark and dreaming. I placed her in the chair, and put a piece of old, yellow silk behind her, something I had bought years before in Paris. It took a long while to get the light to fall just as I wanted it, and to set my easel at the right angle; and all that time she just sat there quietly, staring in front of her, without saying anything. When I was satisfied that I had everything the way I wanted it, I set my canvas up, and began to work.

The picture I started that day needs no description, for most of you have seen it in the Metropolitan Museum, in New York. It is the picture of a girl somewhere in her early 'teens, seated in front of a golden screen. The Museum calls it *Girl In A Black Dress,* but to me it has always been simply Jennie.

I worked in silence, almost in a dream, filled with a strange excitement. So lost was I in what I was doing, that I failed to keep track of the time; I must have been painting well over two hours, when I suddenly saw Jennie droop forward in her chair, and start to slip to the floor. I dropped my brush and ran to her, with my heart in my mouth.

But when I lifted her in my arms, she opened her eyes, and smiled timidly up at me. " I'm tired, Eben," was all she said.

She seemed to me to weigh almost nothing. I laid her down on the bed, with her coat over her; and put some water on the stove to heat for tea. When it was ready I made her drink it, and a little color came back into her cheeks. " I'm better now," she said. " I'm not so cold. I can sit there again, if you want me to."

But of course I didn't want her to. " No," I declared, " it's time for you to rest. You've been the best kind of model; we've done very well, we've got a good start. There's lots of time."

She gave another little sigh, almost like a whisper. " No," she said, " there isn't. But I'll do as you say; I'll rest, if you say so."

Shivering a little, she lay back beneath her coat, with closed eyes, her night-dark hair spread out on my pillow, her hand cold as earth in mine. I stood looking down at her, the narrow curve of the young brow, the long lashes which rested so gently on the cheek beneath them; and I felt my heart contract with a sort of fear, and yet at the same time with delight. Who are you? I thought; and what has brought you here to me? . . . child and stranger, lost and lonely, out of some story in the past? . . .

My hands must have trembled a little, for she opened her eyes and looked gravely up at me. "You're all I have now, Eben," she said.

At my start, half surprise, and half dismay, she let go of my hand, and sat up, huddled under her coat, her thin arms wrapped around her knees. "Except for my aunt," she said, to reassure me. "Only I don't know her very well. She's going to take care of me from now on."

"Well," I said uncomfortably, "that's all right, then, isn't it."

She looked at me beseechingly; it was her turn

to ask for reassurance. " You do want me to come," she asked uncertainly, " don't you? To pose, I mean?

" You don't want me never to come again? "

I couldn't speak, but she must have seen in my face the answer to her doubts, for she smiled, and brushed the hair back from her face with the same gesture I had seen her use that first evening — how many years ago? — in the Mall. " I'll come as soon as I can," she said.

" Jennie — " I began hoarsely.

" Yes, Eben? "

I looked away; after all, what was there to say? Nothing; I did not even know what I had been thinking. " Where does your aunt live? " I asked. At least, I thought, I shall know where she is, and then if I must, I can find her. But she shook her head. " What does it matter where I live? " she said. " You can't come to me.

" I can only come to you."

She spoke sadly, with exquisite gentleness, but with infinite finality. For a moment we looked at each other across a gulf of more than air — a gulf over which no soul had ever passed before, either to go or to return. . . . She made a little, helpless gesture, as though to reach out to me. And then the moment was gone, and she withdrew once more into herself, a stranger, dreaming of something I could not see.

But I knew then that we both knew.

After a while she got up and put on her hat and coat. "Goodbye, Eben," she said. "I'll come back as soon as I can. I'll hurry — truly."

She looked up at me with eyes wide and dark and earnest. "I didn't want you to know," she said.

She turned once, in the doorway. "Try to wait," she whispered.

"Try to wait for me."

CHAPTER 10

ONE must sometimes believe what one cannot understand. That is the method of the scientist as well as the mystic: faced with a universe which must be endless and infinite, he accepts it, although he cannot really imagine it. For there is no picture in our minds of infinity; somewhere, at the furthermost limits of thought, we never fail to plot its end. Yet — if there is no end? Or if, at the end, we are only back at the beginning again? . . .

When Jennie returned, a fortnight later, I realized how much taller she had grown in the last few meetings. She was dressed in a uniform such as young ladies wear at a convent boarding school — a middy blouse, and a skirt which hung almost to her ankles. She came bounding up the stairs, and threw her hat on the bed. "Eben," she cried, "what fun."

For a moment I was thoroughly taken aback, for if I had expected anything at all, it was certainly not that. There was nothing to remind me of the last time I had seen her; in fact, there was nothing of the child about her at all, as far as I could see. On the contrary, she seemed to stand almost within the shadow of vigorous young womanhood. I thought: I must finish my portrait quickly, before it's too late . . .

I couldn't avoid saying, "You've grown, Jennie. And those clothes . . ."

She looked down at herself, and laughed ruefully. "I know," she said. "Aren't they awful? They make us wear them at the convent."

Breaking off suddenly, she looked at me in a startled way. "Oh," she cried; "of course . . . you didn't know . . .

"I'm at St. Mary's now, with Emily. My aunt sent me."

"I suppose I guessed as much," I answered. "Well — I've been waiting for you. We'd better begin."

She took her place in the chair, and I brought out an old black coat of my own to put over the middy blouse. "I can do the dress some other time," I told her. "I won't need you for that."

She sat up very stiff and straight in the chair. "Well," she said with a pout, "aren't you glad to see me?"

It was a very different sitting from the one before, and harder, too. Jenny was restless, and in high spirits; she wanted to stop every few minutes, to talk or to walk around. She was full of her life at school, enchanted with the friendships, the comings and goings, the daily incidents of the convent society — happy at having friends, at having secrets — at being, for the first time in her life, part of a little community. There was the plain-song she had to tell me about; the daily walks to the little green-house, where the girls were allowed to buy fruit from one of the sisters; the little bunches of flowers they gave one another, which they called "bunching"; the convent-school itself, high on its hill above the shining river; and Sister Therese, who taught her mathematics and history, and whose calm, untroubled face had already roused in Jennie's breast the first sharp, sweet experience of love. And then there was Emily, of course, whose secrets and whose room she shared, who exchanged stockings and blouses with her, and on whose dresser there was a picture — but only when nobody would be likely to come in — of a young man in a high collar, with dark eyes and wavy hair, and the printed name beneath it, Mr. John Gilbert.

Yes — Jennie had changed; I even noticed that she had filled out a little. On the whole, I thought it a change for the better. I let her talk on and on, barely listening, my fingers racing in tiny spurts over the canvas, trying at their best speed to follow my eyes; and my eyes, in turn, searching for what they could not see — not only what was there, but what had been, and what would some day be. I felt that I was truly working against time, and felt myself carried forward on a wave of exultation as the picture bloomed under the brush, as I saw, each time I stepped away from it, its growing strength, its gathering beauty.

We stopped at noon for a bite of lunch, although I would gladly have gone on without any. But that would never do for Jennie. It turned out that she had been planning all along to cook lunch for me, on my little gas stove; and that she had even taken lessons in cooking in school. Unfortunately, there was nothing in the studio, as far as I could see, for her to cook.

"I have some sardines," I said, "and some cheese, and crackers, and milk. I'm sorry, Jennie. You see, I didn't know you were coming."

She laughed happily. "That's all I can cook, anyhow," she said. "I could cook an egg, but it doesn't matter. I'll cook the cheese."

And she did, actually, get the cheese to melt, though not without some scorching, and a smell of burning that I was afraid would bring up Mrs. Jekes. After it was melted, she dropped it on the crackers, and there it lay, altogether inedible, and more and more like rubber. I ate a few sardines, and after a while, she did, too. "Isn't this fun?" she said.

And of course, to her, it was. For if Emily had Mr. Gilbert, Jennie had me — her own exciting secret, to be shared in whispers if she felt like it, or held close and inviolable to her breast. Everyone has a secret at that age; a special secret, a private secret — for everything between earth and sky is part of the one great, general secret which young hearts whisper to one another. New sights — new sounds — new meanings — new joys and fears — her heart, which through her childhood was all one color, has turned into a kaleidoscope, made up of shining fragments which fall at each turn of the glass into ever newer, more breath-taking patterns. Emily . . . Sister Therese . . . plain-song and flowers . . . and finally, myself — all her own, her own private secret, which no one else can know, until she tells.

"The girls keep asking me about you," she confessed. "But I won't tell them anything. Except . . ." she considered a moment . . . "that you're very handsome . . ." And she began to count off on her fingers.

"Jennie," I said; "don't be silly."

". . . and that you're a great artist; and that you nearly starved to death . . ."

She smiled at me shyly. "They loved that part of it," she declared. "They thought it was very romantic."

"Good God," I said.

"Well, they did," she insisted. "And they think it's romantic my coming to see you like this, too."

Her voice was still full of laughter, but her cheeks were pink, and she kept her head bent.

"Perhaps it is," I replied a little grimly. "But we've got work to do, and if you've finished with that last bit of milk, we might begin."

Her eyes flew to my face in dismay. "You're not angry, are you, Eben?" she faltered. "I was only joking."

"Of course I'm not angry," I said a little too gruffly, and stood up. "Let's get back to work — shall we?"

She took her place again in a somewhat chastened mood; but she couldn't stay quiet for long. "Eben," she said.

"Mmm?"

"I didn't really say you were handsome."

But that didn't comfort me much.

"I wish I had nicer clothes to wear," she said after a while. "We have a blue dress with a guimpe, for Sundays, and we have to wear long white veils in church. Emily's fell off, the last time; she didn't pin it on right, she was in such a hurry, and she got a whole day's silence."

Receiving no reply to this bit of information, she went on to other things. "I like some of my lessons," she said. "I like things like science, and math. But I don't like history. It makes me feel too sad.

"I have a funny mind, I guess."

I was holding one brush in my teeth while I worked with another, and I mumbled something in reply.

" You have a funny mind, too," she said.

" Perhaps I have," I agreed absently. " Perhaps I have. Just turn your head a little to the right — "

" Eben," she began presently in a queer, breathless voice, " do you think sometimes people can know what lies ahead? I mean — what's going to happen to them? "

But I was working, and thinking only of what I was doing. Otherwise I would have stopped — and thought — and perhaps have been too much troubled by the question to make any answer at all. As it was, I only half heard it; and I answered without thinking.

" Nonsense," I said.

Jennie was silent for a moment; then, " I don't know," she said slowly. " I'm not so sure. You know how you feel sad about things sometimes — things that haven't happened. Perhaps they're things that are going to happen. Perhaps we know it, and are just afraid to admit it to ourselves. Why couldn't you, Eben — if you could see ahead — feel sorry for what was coming? Only you wouldn't know it was coming, you'd call it worry, or something."

I heard it, but I wasn't really paying attention. "You sound like the White Queen," I said.

"The White Queen?"

"The one in Alice," I told her. "She hollered first, and stuck herself afterwards."

"Oh," said Jennie in a small voice. Even with the little mind I had to attend to anything but my painting, I could tell that I had hurt her.

"All right," she said. "I won't talk any more."

And for the remainder of the sitting, she sat there silent and unsmiling, drawn back once more into herself, dreaming and distant. But I was too busy to try to explain; and besides, it did the picture good. When the light began to fail, I put down my brush, and took a deep breath.

"I think I've got it, Jennie," I said.

There was no answer; she seemed to be half asleep. I went quietly down the hall to the wash room, to freshen up; I doubt if I was away for more than a minute or so. But when I got back, Jennie was gone.

She left a note for me, on the bed. "Eben dear," it said; "I'll be back again some day. But not soon. In the spring, I think.

Jennie."

CHAPTER 11

EVEN before I telephoned out to the school, I knew what the answer would be. "I'm sorry; there is no one here by that name." I didn't ask them to go back over their files; I knew what the answer would be to that, too.

So there it was.

I must try to describe, if I can, my state of mind in the weeks which followed. I knew that what I had been asked to believe, was impossible; yet I believed it. And at the same time, I was afraid. The fact that my fears were formless, that I did not know what I feared, made it all the worse; for waking or sleeping, nothing frightens us more than the unknown.

I do not know which was harder to bear — the feeling of being afraid, or the sudden sense of desolation which swept down upon me after Jennie had left. She was gone beyond the farthest sea; and there was nowhere I could even look for her.

It made the world around me seem curiously empty — silent, and empty, like the wooden belly of a violin on which nothing is being played. One note would bring it all to life; one note would make an instrument of it. But the note is not played; no one touches it. It remains an empty box.

At first, I was absorbed in my own helplessness; and at the same time, baffled by it. Never before had it occurred to me to ask myself why the sun should rise each morning on a new day instead of upon the old day over again; or to wonder how much of what I did was really my own to do. It may be that here on this earth we are not grateful enough for our ignorance, and our innocence. We think that there is only one road, one direction — forward; and we accept it, and press on. We think of God, we think of the mystery of the universe, but we do not think about it very much, and we do not really believe that it is a mystery, or that we could not understand it if it were explained to us. Perhaps that is because when all is said and done, we do not really believe in God. In our hearts, we are convinced that it is our world, not His.

How stupid of us. Yet we are created stupid — innocent and ignorant; and it is this ignorance alone which makes it possible for us to live on this earth, in comfort, among the mysteries. Since we do not know, and cannot guess, we need not bother our heads too much to understand. It is innocence which wakes us each morning to a new day, a fresh day, another day in a long chain of days; it is ignorance which makes each of our acts appear to be a new one, and the result of an exercise of will. Without such ignorance, we should perish of terror, frozen and immobile; or, like the old saints who learned the true name of God, go up in a blaze of unbearable vision.

I went back to work; and there, before my easel again, I got back a little of my peace of mind. I realized that I was still anchored to earth, and that no matter what God was about, if I was to live, it would have to be by my own efforts. Little by little the sense of being helpless, the fog of fear, burned itself out of my heart, and left me clear, and grateful — and lonely.

It was this loneliness, which I had not expected, and to which I was unused, which kept me from taking the finished portrait to Mr. Mathews at once. It was all I had of Jennie, all I had to remind me that she was really there in the world; and I could not bring myself to part with it. I found that I kept waiting for her to come back; some part of me which had always been whole and satisfied, was suddenly so no longer; something was missing.

Mrs. Jekes found me talking to the portrait one day. I don't know what I was saying — probably something I had said before, to the real Jennie. She came quietly up behind me, with a duster in her hand, and stood looking over my shoulder. "Well," she said; "well."

It startled me; and disturbed me, too. I moved away, trying to look as though I hadn't been talking out loud to myself, as though it were all a mistake, as though it was something quite natural. But Mrs. Jekes wasn't fooled. "That's the girl who's been visiting you," she said, and her voice was full of malice.

"That's your sweetheart."

I whirled on her in a rage. "You're a fool," I shouted. I wanted to strike her, to push her out of the room. But she stood her ground, and gave me back look for look. " It isn't me is the fool," she said bitterly.

She moved to the door with a sort of bleak dignity. " You can always leave this house if you've a mind to," she said. " There's others will be glad to take your place."

And she added, as she went out,

" You're not a gentleman."

I wanted to run after her and tell her that I was leaving, that I was leaving at once . . . but before I had taken two steps, I halted in dismay. For I realized that I couldn't leave. This was Jennie's room: this was where she had sat, where we had had lunch together, this was what she loved to come back to — how could I leave it? It was full of memories of her.

And besides — if I moved — how would she ever find me again?

I closed the door gently, and turned slowly back

into the room again. I'd have to stay; I'd have to tell Mrs. Jekes that I was sorry for what I had said. It put a bitter taste in my mouth. I took Jennie's picture, and turned it to the wall. I didn't want to think about her for a while.

Just the same, I thought about very little else. That was early in March; it was early in April before I saw her again. At least, I know now that I saw her; though I wasn't sure at the time. It was only for a moment; and I had no chance to talk to her.

It was at the gallery, at an exhibition of some of Jerry Farnsworth's things, with one or two of Helen Sawyer's landscapes hanging with them — scenes of the Cape, the crossing at North Truro, an old house, and a painting of the Pamet where it flows past the town landing at Truro. There had been a good crowd in to see them, quite a lot of people; and I had gone back into Mr. Mathews' little office in the rear of the gallery, to talk to Miss Spinney. She had sold the flower-piece at a profit; and she was feeling friendly, and pleased with herself.

"Adams," she said, after she had greeted me, "tell me something: what is it makes a painter? A man will starve all his life, go around with holes in his pants and his toes sticking out of his boots, and still all he wants to do is slap some paint on a yard of canvas. Who's crazy — him or us? What did you do with the twenty-five dollars you got off us the last time?"

"I spent it," I said.

"Sure," she agreed; "I didn't think you'd bought a bond with it. Only, why not a new coat, or a pair of shoes?"

I looked down at my scuffed and broken shoes, and shrugged my shoulders. I didn't see what business it was of hers. "Oh well," I said, "I could get them shined, and they'd look all right. That is, if I ever thought about it."

“Have they got any soles left on them at all?” she asked.

I grinned at her, but I kept my feet planted firmly on the floor, for I knew it would be like her to pick one of them up the way a blacksmith does when he wants to shoe a horse. “I didn’t know you cared,” I murmured.

“Don’t be an ass,” she said. But a slow blush ran up her neck, up over the clean, strong lines of her jaw.

“All right,” I said, feeling a little silly, “next time throw in a pair of shoes with the price.”

She swore at me like a truck driver; and I went out to look for Mr. Mathews.

I didn’t see him at first, for he was at the door saying goodbye to one of the customers. The gallery was nearly empty by this time; a few people were still standing in front of Farnsworth’s “Rest After Work,” but otherwise the big room was deserted. The Sawyers were over in a far corner, near the door; and I started toward them.

Like all galleries, the room itself was only dimly lighted; the pictures on the wall seemed to have their own light, to give out reflections of sun and sea, or morning sky and noonday earth, which made the air of the room itself seem shadowy and vague. I thought I heard Miss Spinney come out of the office behind me, and turned back for a moment. But there was no one there. When I turned around again, it seemed to me that my heart stopped beating.

There was somebody in front of the Sawyers — a young girl, dressed in a middy blouse, and a skirt which hung almost to her ankles. She was standing directly in front of the picture of the Pamet; that much I could see across the room, in the shadowy light; but no more. She had her hands to her face; and I thought that she was weeping.

"Jennie," I said; or perhaps I only thought I

said it. I tried to move, to get across to her, but my legs were like lead. It was all I could do to put one foot before the other. I could feel the slow, heavy surge of my heart, as I kept trying to breathe, catching at my breath, the way you do in a gale.

She lifted her head, and for a moment I had a glimpse of her face, wet and shiny with tears. And then — she was gone. It was just as simple as that. Perhaps she went out through the door — I don't know. Mr. Mathews, coming in at that moment, bent aside as though to let someone pass. Perhaps it was Jennie.

He came across the floor to me, smiling; but when he saw my face, his expression changed. "Good heavens, Mr. Adams," he cried, "is anything the matter? You look sick, man."

I shook my head; I couldn't say anything. I passed him without speaking, and stumbled out of the door. He looked after me in bewilderment.

I left him there wondering what had happened to me.

There were only the usual passers-by in the street. I hadn't expected there would be anyone else.

CHAPTER 12

SPRING was early that year; the rainy winds blew themselves out before the end of April. One day the grass in the Park smelt sweet and fresh, and a robin sang on the lawn below the Mall. From then on, the sky seemed made of another blue, and the clouds, too, were a different white, with tones of yellow in them. Yellow is the true color of spring, not green; the new grass, the clouds, the misty, sunny air, the sticky buds like little feathers on the trees, all are mixed with yellow tone, with the haze of sun and earth and water. Green is for summer; blue, for fall.

The city comes up dreaming from the winter, its high roofs seem to melt in the air. The wind blows from the south, across Jersey; it smells sweet, it brings the smell of earth with it. People move more slowly, there is a gentleness about them, the cold is not yet out of their bones, they warm themselves in the sun. The days are longer, and the shadows are not as deep; evenings come down almost imperceptibly, there are long twilights, the dusk is peaceful, and the sounds of evening are tranquil and comforting. Summer lies ahead, the summer of the heart; it is coming, it has been caught sight of, it is on the way, bringing flowers and sea-bathing.

Summer is the worst time of all to be alone. Then earth is warm and lovely, free to go about in; and always somewhere in the distance there is a place where two people might be happy if only they were together. It is in the spring that one dreams of such places; one thinks of the summer which is coming, and the heart dreams of its friend.

Now in the Park I began to see people walking together, slowly, arm in arm, not hurrying as they did in winter, but taking time to talk to each other, stopping a moment to laugh at the children, or to watch the swans on the lake. When summer came, they would be together still; they could enjoy the spring. But for me, it was different. I had no way of knowing when I should see Jennie again. And as the days passed, I missed her more and more.

There is one thing about distance: that no matter how far away it is, it can be reached. It is over there, beyond the Jersey hills — one can drive to it — it is north, among the pines, or eastward to the sea. It is never yesterday, or tomorrow. That is another, and a crueller distance; there is no way to get there.

Yet, though I missed her, though I could not reach her, I was not altogether without her. For I found that my memory had grown sharper; or else it was beginning to play tricks on me. It was not so much that I began to live in the past, as that the past began to take on more and more the clarity, the actual form of the present, and to intrude itself into my daytime thoughts. The present, on the contrary, seemed to grow a little hazy, to begin to slip away from me . . . so many things reminded me of her. And then I would be seized by memory so urgent that what I remembered seemed almost more real to me than what was before me.

Where others dreamed ahead that spring, toward the summer, I dreamed backward into the past. Sights, sounds, and smells, all served that journey well — the smell of scorching, the sound of wood — perhaps a shovel? — scraped along the pavement; the hoot of a tugboat in the river. At nightfall the shrill, sad voices of children, floating in through my window, brought back to me another evening, in the mist, in the Park, and a child walking beside me down the long avenue of empty benches, skipping along on one foot, hopping over the chalk marks . . . "*Do you know the game I like to play best? It's a wishing game.*" Or on a sunny morning, beside the lake on which the boats were lazily drifting, I'd suddenly find myself entranced and motionless, seeing in front of me not the blue, dancing water, but the white, shining ice and the skaters, feeling the cold wind on my cheeks again, and Jennie's arm in mine, so firm and light. . . . Or coming home in the afternoon, I'd hurry up the stairs with a beating heart, because she might be there — remembering so clearly the first time she had come to see me, in her little velvet dress with the muff. "*I thought maybe you wanted me to come,*" she had said.

Such was my state of mind those early days of spring — neither happy nor unhappy; dreaming, and waiting. I didn't want very much, or hope for very much — just to see her again, and to be with her once more. I tried not to think about the summer, or, indeed, about the future at all; — how could I? I left that to her, just as I had left the past to her. Why we had met, or how it had come about, I did not know. I still do not know. I only know that we were meant to be together, that the strands of her life were woven in with mine; and that even time and the world could not part us altogether. Not then. Not ever.

What is it which makes a man and a woman know that they, of all other men and women in the world, belong to each other? Is it no more than chance and meeting? no more than being alive together in the world at the same time? Is it only a curve of the throat, a line of the chin, the way the eyes are set, a way of speaking? Or is it something deeper and stranger, something beyond meeting, something beyond chance and fortune? Are there others, in other times of the world, whom we would have loved, who would have loved us? Is there, perhaps, one soul among all others — among all who have lived, the endless generations, from world's end to world's end — who must love us or die? And whom we must love, in turn — whom we must seek all our lives long — headlong and homesick — until the end?

By May I had no money left at all, and so I took the portrait down to Mr. Mathews. I hated to give it up, but there was no help for it; I needed money for rent, and for more paints, and canvas. I was still getting some of my meals at the Alhambra, although I had finished my work there; the picnic over the bar seemed to please the customers, and Mr. Moore didn't mind my having one free meal a day, as long as I didn't eat too much. As a matter of fact, he was thinking of getting up a fancy menu with an illustrated cover — possibly a picture of the restaurant, with himself standing in the doorway. Gus wanted me to get his cab into it, too. I didn't mind; an artist works for his meals one way or another.

Gus helped me bring the picture downtown in his cab, and went along with me to see that I wasn't cheated. We carried it into the gallery together, and set it up on the table in the office in the rear. Then we stepped aside, and let Mr. Mathews look at it.

He didn't say anything for a long while. At first I thought that he was disappointed, and my heart sank; but then I saw that he was really very much moved. He had grown a little pale; his eyes first widened, and then narrowed; and he kept stroking the palm of one hand with the fingers of the other. " Well," he said. " Well.

" Yes."

I began to feel excited, too. Up till then, I doubt if I had really looked at the picture myself with any sort of critical eye. There, in my room, it had been so much a part of me; I could still feel the brush strokes in my fingers . . . and besides, it was Jennie, it was all I had of her. . . . But here, in the gallery, seeing it as Mr. Mathews was seeing it, I could realize for the first time what I had done. It made me feel proud, and at the same time humble.

After a while Miss Spinney came in and joined us. She didn't say anything for a minute; and then she took a long breath. "Well, Adams," she said in a strangely gentle voice, "that's it, all right."

Mr. Mathews cleared his throat. "Yes," he said, "that's it. That's what I meant. It's . . . it's . . ." He seemed unable to continue. It was Gus who spoke up for him.

"She's a honey, Mack," he said. "I don't noways blame you."

And turning to Miss Spinney, he added in an easy tone,

" Treat him right, ma'am, on account of he's a friend of mine."

" I'll keep it in mind," said Miss Spinney.

She and Mr. Mathews went outside, to talk it over; and Gus edged up to me and gave me a nudge with his elbow. " I think they like it, Mack," he whispered.

" Yes," I said; " I think they do."

" Well, don't be too easy on them," he said. " Ask for fifty, right off."

" It's worth twice that," I said.

Gus' jaw dropped. " No," he croaked. " Go on. I wouldn't of believed it."

Mr. Mathews and Miss Spinney came back again, looking solemn; and Mr. Mathews settled down to business. " Mr. Adams," he began —

" Why so formal? " said Miss Spinney. " He's in the family."

" Well, then — Eben," said Mr. Mathews, swallowing, " I won't try to disguise my feelings from you. You have given me a great surprise. I am powerfully moved. This picture . . . well . . . I don't like to use the word masterpiece, but just the same . . ."

"Get on with it, Henry," said Miss Spinney.

"Yes," said Mr. Mathews hurriedly. "Quite. The point is, that we don't want to buy it. No," he said, holding up his hand as he saw my face fall — "it's not for the reason you think. The reason is, that I honestly don't know what it's worth."

"Well," I said, "what do you think it's worth?"

"That depends," he answered, "on who buys it. The market isn't very good just at the moment, for individual collectors. But if the museum were to take it —"

"Yes?" I said.

"It might bring more than a thousand dollars," he said.

I heard Gus give a gulp beside me. "What I want to do," continued Mr. Mathews — "what we want to do — is to take it on consignment, and then do the very best we can for it. And as an advance — " he cleared his throat nervously — " as an advance, I can let you have two hundred dollars . . ."

"Henry," said Miss Spinney ominously.

"Three hundred," amended Mr. Mathews unhappily.

Then Gus found his voice again. "Take it, Mack," he said hoarsely; and gave me a shove.

I went home in his cab, leaning back on the cushion, and looking out proudly at my city, which seemed to me to return my look with joy. Through the open window in front, I could see the back of Gus' head; I noticed that he had turned the flag down on his meter, and that the meter was ticking. Well, why not? I was a rich man. But just the same, I was surprised; and it surprised me that Gus wasn't saying anything. His silence wasn't natural; it wasn't like him.

He left me at my house, and took my fare without a word. When I tried to thank him for helping me, he looked away. "Forget it," he said. "It don't signify."

He took his hands off the wheel, and stared at them helplessly, as though in some way or other they had disappointed him. Then he let them drop again.

"I couldn't do nothing for you, Mack," he said. "And that's the truth."

CHAPTER 13

EARLY next morning, in the bright spring sunshine, Jennie came back to me. I heard her voice in the hall, and had only time to slip into my coat, before she was up the stairs and in at the door. She had a little suit-case in her hand; she dropped it just inside the doorway, and came flying across the room, and kissed me.

It was the most natural thing in the world. We

held each other out at arm's length and looked at each other, smiling, and not saying anything. We couldn't have spoken . . . The whole sunny, sweet-smelling spring morning had come in with her.

She was older — I saw that at once; a young lady now, dressed in a travelling suit; she even had gloves on. She was breathless, but only from running up the stairs, or from happiness; her brown eyes never faltered as they searched my face. I took a deep breath. "Jennie," I said; "I've missed you."

"I know," she answered. "I've missed you, too. And it's been longer for me." She drew her hands away from mine with sudden gravity. "I'm not in school any more," she said.

"I know," I said. "I can see."

She turned slowly on her heel, and looked around the room with simple joy. "How I've dreamed of this, Eben," she said; "I can't tell you.

The nights I've lain awake, thinking of this room . . ."

"I know," I said.

"Do you?" she answered gently. "No, I don't think so."

She stood there, looking around her, and slowly taking off her gloves; and I looked around, too, and wished the room were more in order. I went over to smooth the bed a little, but she stopped me. "No," she said; "don't touch it. Do you remember how I wanted to tidy up for you once, when I was little? Let me do it now. And show me where the coffee is . . . Poor Eben — I did get you up so early. Go and dress yourself, and then we'll have breakfast, and I'll tell you all that's happened."

"But Jennie," I said, "if we have so little time . . ."

"We have a whole long day," she answered breathlessly. "And — and a little more."

I went along down the hall to the washroom,

and left Jennie to tidy up, as she wanted. I thought I saw Mrs. Jekes on the landing below, but I didn't pay much attention to her; I was too happy, the day was too lovely . . . a whole long day, and a little more. What did that mean — a little more? I cut myself twice, shaving.

Jennie had learned how to make a bed, and how to make coffee. I hardly knew my room when I got back to it: my work-table was laid with a clean towel, and my two cups, one of them with a broken handle, and the coffee pot, stood side by side, along with a pat of butter I'd had out on the window sill, and some bread she had toasted on a fork over the gas burner. There was a good smell in the air. We sat down together, hand in hand, to our breakfast.

I told her about the picture; and her fingers tightened on mine. "Oh, but that's grand," she cried. "That's wonderful, Eben. Aren't you happy?"

She was silent for a moment, thinking about something. "Eben," she said at last, "let's do something special—shall we? To celebrate? Because I haven't really very long to stay with you. You see . . . I'm being sent abroad—to France—to a finishing school—for two years."

"Jennie," I cried.

"I know," she said quickly. "I don't want to go; but I guess I have to. And anyhow—it won't seem very long. And then . . ."

"And then?" I asked.

"I'm going to hurry," she said earnestly. "And then some day I'll be as old as you."

"I'm twenty-eight, Jennie," I said gravely. She nodded her head.

"I know it," she replied. "And so will I be . . . then."

"But not when you come back from France," I said.

"No," she agreed. "There'll be a long time still, after that."

She held my hand tight. "I'm going to hurry, though," she said. "I've got to."

For a moment she seemed to be lost in thought, her head bent, her eyes hidden under their long lashes. Then she roused herself, and sat up with a smile. "Let's go on a picnic, Eben," she said. "Somewhere in the country — for the whole day —

"It's something we've never done before."

Something we'd never done before — as though we'd ever done very much of anything. But she didn't have to urge me. A whole day in the country, in the warm spring weather, together . . . "Yes," I said, "yes. That's what we'll do." She could hardly wait for me to finish my coffee; we hurried down the stairs and out into the street, hand in hand; and the bright sunny morning fell on us like an armful of flowers.

Gus was in his cab, at the corner. When he saw me with Jennie, he took his hat off, and looked frightened. I don't believe he had ever thought she was real, or ever expected to see her. I went up to the cab, and opened the door. "Gus," I said, "we're going on a picnic. We're going out into the country for the day . . . somewhere . . . anywhere. I want you to take us. How much will it cost?"

He twisted his hat in his hands, and tried to smile; he seemed to be having some trouble in swallowing. "Now listen, Mack," he said; "now listen . . ."

"It doesn't matter what it costs," I said, and helped Jennie into the cab.

What was the good of being rich, if I couldn't do what I liked?

Gus looked back once or twice, as though to make sure that we were really there. "So it's a fact," he said finally, more to himself than to me; and in a kind of awe. "Well — "

"Where do you want to go, Mack?"

I waved him forward. "Wherever it's green," I said. "Wherever it's country."

I don't know where we went, but it was green and lovely. It was somewhere north of the city — perhaps in Westchester. It took us about an hour to get there. We left the cab by the roadside, and climbed a fence, and ran across a field with a cow in it. The cow didn't notice us. We climbed a little hill, among some trees. Jennie was flushed and breathless, and full of laughter; she and I ran ahead, and Gus came after us.

At noon we sat together on a warm stone wall in the sun at the edge of a meadow, and near a little wood. There were yellow dandelions in the grass, and the air was sweet as honey. We had some sandwiches along — lettuce and bread for

Jennie, sausage for Gus and me. We ate our sandwiches, and drank some beer out of cans. It was the first beer Jennie had ever tasted; she didn't like it, she said it tasted bitter.

Gus and Jennie did most of the talking. He told her how he had tried to find her once; and how he had helped me sell the picture; and she told him please to take good care of me, and not to let anything happen. I didn't talk very much; I felt drowsy in the sun, I kept wishing Arne were there, too; I kept thinking about what it would be like some day when we were all together.

Jennie sat on the wall beside me, her head against my shoulder. She had twined a yellow dandelion in her hair; it gave out a fresh, weedy fragrance. The sky was robin's egg blue; I heard a bird singing in the woods. I was happy — happier than I had ever been before, happier than I've ever been since.

Gus left us after lunch, and went back to the

cab, to take a nap. Then Jennie too grew silent, resting against me, dreamy and content. After a while, I felt her stir, and draw a long, uneven breath. "What are you thinking, Jennie?" I asked.

She answered slowly and gently, "I'm thinking how beautiful the world is, Eben; and how it keeps on being beautiful — no matter what happens to us. The spring comes year after year, for us, or Egypt; the sun goes down in the same green, lovely sky; the birds sing . . . for us, or yesterday . . . or for tomorrow. It was never made for anything but beauty, Eben — whether we lived now, or long ago."

"Tomorrow," I said. "But when is tomorrow, Jennie?"

"Does it matter?" she asked. "It's always. This was tomorrow — once.

"Promise me you'll never forget."

I quoted softly:

" Where I come from,
Nobody knows,
And where I'm going,
Everything goes."

She took it up with a little cry of surprise:

" The wind blows,
The sea flows —
And God knows.

" I think He knows, Eben," she said.

And she lifted her lips, trusting and innocent, to mine.

Later we walked in the faint green of the woods, through the shadow of branches, over the ferns and the moss. We found a little brook, and violets hidden among their leaves. Jennie stopped to pick them; she made a tiny bunch, to carry home. " It's to remember today," she said.

The sun began to sink in the west; the shadows fell around us. It grew chilly; we turned, and started home.

CHAPTER 14

I HAD one clear day of happiness, and I shall never forget it. Even the miserable ending to it cannot change its quality in my memory; for everything that Jennie and I did was good, and unhappiness came only from the outside. Not many — lovers or friends — can say as much. For friends and lovers are quick to wound, quicker than strangers, even; the heart that opens itself to the world, opens itself to sorrow.

I don't think that we spoke of the question of where Jennie was to stay that night. She was sailing in the morning (on the Mauretania, I remember she told me — how strange it was to hear the old name again) and we both seemed to take it for granted that we'd stay together until then.

We had supper at the Alhambra, at a little table near the bar, where she could see my mural, and then we walked home together in the quiet evening. It was cool, the air was still, and in the green west the evening star hung like a lantern over the city.

Those are the scenes, the memories, with which I comfort myself. The spring comes year after year, she had said, and tomorrow is always. When at last there was no tomorrow any more, I remembered yesterday. Yesterday is always, too.

She told me that she had been at the gallery that day of the exhibition, when I thought I had seen her; and that she had been crying. "I don't know why," she said. "It was a picture of a river, and some little hills across on the other side — the Pamet, it was called. And all of a sudden I felt that I knew it, and that it was a sad place — and I found myself crying. I wanted to come to you, but I couldn't; I had to go back. I was unhappy for a while, and then I forgot it."

She put her hand in mine; it was trembling a little. "I'm sorry that you asked me," she said. "I didn't want to remember it."

I turned her hand over, and patted it. "It's a funny little river, Jennie," I said, "and not sad at all. It comes in from the bay, and it's not very deep. The children play there, and the bitterns croak in the reeds at night. And at low tide, everybody goes out and digs for clams."

She smiled uncertainly. "I know," she said. "I'm being silly. Don't let's talk about it any more. Tell me about Paris, instead — you were there, weren't you? Is it very lovely? My school is in

Passy — is that near where you were? Tell me what to see, and what to do — so that some day we'll have done it all together. . . ."

We sat on the edge of the bed, and talked for a long time. I told her about Arne, about the Atelier Dufoix, about the Clos des Lilas, where we used to go sometimes when we had money, and the little bistro on the Rue du Bac where we went when we didn't. She listened to me hungrily, seeing it all ahead of her. " Oh Eben," she said; " it's going to be such fun."

We even planned what we'd do together. I remembered a room on the Île St. Louis, where a friend of mine had lived — a room like the prow of a ship, butting its way up the Seine, and the river pouring by on both sides, under the windows. I promised to take her to the Luxembourg, to the Quai des Marinières, and to the Fair at Neuilly — I promised to dance with her in the Place Pigalle on Bastille Day — and to take her out into the

Forest of St. Cloud in the spring, to drink new wine under the trees. " It's going to be such fun," she said.

It was late when Mrs. Jekes knocked on the door. I think I shall remember the sound of it all my life. When death comes at last, I expect he'll sound like that, too.

Even before the door opened, I think I had an idea of what was coming. She stood in the doorway, a still, wintry figure, her hands folded, as always, across her stomach. " Oh no," she said; " oh no. Not in my house, not at night, you won't. There's a limit to everything, my friends. I've run a decent place all my life, and I mean to keep it so."

And pointing a white, shaking finger at Jennie, she cried suddenly,

" Get out."

I was too startled even to speak. I seemed to freeze up inside; perhaps it was just as well, for otherwise there's no telling what I might have done. Jennie got up from the bed, slowly, as though in a dream; she turned her frightened face away from me, so that I shouldn't see how ashamed she was. She went quietly over to the chair where she had laid her hat and coat.

"I'm sorry, Eben," she faltered. "I didn't think . . ."

"Get out," said Mrs. Jekes.

I found my voice then. "Be still," I cried to her; and to Jennie: "Don't listen . . . don't listen to her."

But Jennie shook her head. "No," she said; "no — it's too late now: it's been said. It couldn't ever not be said again."

She took up her hat and coat, and stooped to pick up the little suit-case which lay by the door where she had dropped it that morning. Mrs. Jekes moved aside to let her pass. She went by her without a glance, but she turned in the doorway, and looked back at me — a look so full of longing, of love, and of trust, that it was like a hand laid for a moment against my cheek. It was that look, more than anything else, which kept me from rushing after her.

"Goodbye, Eben," she said clearly. "I'll be back again some day — But not like this. Not ever again like this. Not until we can be together always."

Mrs. Jekes watched her go. She followed her down the stairs; I heard her footsteps grow fainter and fainter down the stairs.

CHAPTER 15

I MOVED out of Mrs. Jekes' house after that; and since summer was not far off, I decided to join Arne on the Cape at once. Mr. Mathews and Miss Spinney said goodbye to me like old friends; Mr. Mathews gave me a little folding easel which had belonged to Fromkes, and Miss Spinney gave me a bottle of brandy — to keep, as she put it, the fog out of my fingers. "I want another flower-piece," she declared; "a two-and-a-half by four;

and a church. I'm sort of fond of churches, the little white ones, with the big steeples. Goodbye, and God bless you. Don't drown yourself in the sea."

"What would I want to drown myself in the sea for?" I asked.

"I don't know," she answered. "Men are fools enough to do anything. Personally, I don't trust the sea. I wouldn't go within fifty miles of it."

"You're tough," I said. "The sea would never get you."

She looked at me with a strange expression; I saw the red start to creep up over her chin. "It's the tough ones drown easy," she said, and turned away.

Mr. Mathews walked to the door with me; he kept reaching up every now and then to pat me on the back. "Goodbye, my boy," he said, "goodbye. I'm glad you came to me; we'll do big things together. You've earned a rest; now enjoy it. But remember — no landscapes. Leave the dunes to Eastwood."

"I want to do the fishermen," I said.

"Fishermen," he echoed doubtfully; "well . . ."

"In the traps," I said, "in the early morning, with the fish churning in the nets."

Mr. Mathews looked at me gloomily. "Listen," he said. "There are enough fish in the world."

He sighed heavily. "But not enough women," he added.

Gus took me to my train. "Take care of yourself, Mack," he said. "Don't do anything I wouldn't do." I had Jennie's violets in a paper bag in my pocket; they were withered by now, but they still retained a little of their fragrance. My paints and canvases and my easel were in one bundle, and my clothes were in another. The train went at midnight, the great office buildings were dark as we drove down to the station. I kept thinking of how Jennie had been there in the cab with me only the day before.

I knew that I'd see her again, and I told Gus so. "Sure," he said; "sure. Why not? You don't want to be too wise in this world, Mack, because there's always something happens you don't expect. You take my own people, now—they thought they weren't going to get out of Egypt. But they got out all right. And why? So they could write the Bible.

"They couldn't have guessed that."

"They didn't have to guess it," I said.

"I know," said Gus; "you mean Somebody told them. Well—what did He tell them? That's what I want to know."

"I thought He made it clear," I said.

"Not to me," said Gus. "I'm still trying to figure it out. And the way I figure it, is like this: whatever it was, it was good news, on account of the only bad news would be that what we knew was all there was."

I started to pull out some money to pay him for the ride, but he waved it away. "Forget it," he said. "The flag wasn't down. You've done plenty for me."

"Goodbye, Gus," I said. "I'll see you in the fall."

"Sure," he agreed. "Drop me a postal."

I hesitated a moment before picking up my bags. "You think God is trying to tell me something?" I asked, half in earnest.

"I wouldn't put it past Him," said Gus.

"But what?" I cried.

He shook his head. "I wouldn't know," he said.

I came down into Provincetown the next afternoon. The moment we crossed the bridge at Bourne, and I breathed the warm, sunny fragrance of scrub pine and broom, I felt the old peace of summer flow into me. Lilac was out in the Yarmouth yards and doorways, and in Brewster the juice-pear and the wild plum had opened their blossoms, white as snow. The marshes at Wellfleet were all a silvery green; and beyond Truro, there was the bay, still and shining, bluer than a bluebird's wing, with Plymouth clear, dark, and distant on the horizon.

Arne was waiting for me; he had a room in the west end of town, down near Furtado's boat yard, and he took me there to wash up and get settled. I went to the window, and drew in a deep breath of the past. How well I remembered it. The old weedy, fishy smell rose from the tide; the gulls were circling and crying, out in the harbor; and on the sand below, Manuel was hammering at the white hull of a lobsterman. The schooner *Mary P. Goulart* was in harbor, along with most of the fisheries' fleet; and I saw John Worthington's tunaman, the *Bocage,* come chugging in across the blue water from the North Truro nets, kicking up a little foam at her bows. Slowly and peacefully sky and water deepened; the sun went down over Peaked Hill Bars, and the ruby light came on at Wood End, and the white light at the Point.

We walked down to the fish wharf, past Dyer's hardware store and Page's Garage, past the post office, and the little square with its great elms. The summer visitors hadn't begun to arrive yet, and the town was quiet, with only its own people in the streets. Dark faced fishermen lounged in the doorways, talking together in their own language, half argot and half Portuguese; and the girls went by, two by two in the dusk, hatless and laughing. We stopped in at Taylor's for supper, and I ordered a chowder, the way they make it down there. I wanted to hear the Provincetown news: — who was teaching that year, and how the classes were shaping up, whether Jerry Farnsworth had his old studio, and whether Tom Blakeman was going to take a class in etching again. And then, of course, Arne had to hear about the portrait. When I told him that Mr. Mathews hoped to sell it to a museum some day, he flung out his hands in horror.

"Don't have it, Eben," he thundered. "Never allow it. A museum? The death of the soul."

"Sure," I said. "Like Innes, or Chase."

"They're dead," he answered. "That's all past and done with."

"Is it?" I asked. "I'm not so sure."

"Good God," he bellowed earnestly; "the past is behind us. What?"

"There's still Rembrandt," I said, "and Van Gogh. We're not quite done with them yet. . . . The past isn't behind us, Arne — it's all around us. And down here, on the Cape, is where one onght to feel it most — where the years follow each other like tides in the Pamet, and the boats come in each day with the same fish they had before."

I smiled at him across the table. "I'm only beginning to think about things like that," I said.

"Well," he said unhappily, "I wish you

wouldn't. The artist ought not to think so much, it's bad for his color sense."

And with that, we plunged into the old debate, and for the rest of the meal the talk was all of color and line, symbol, form, and mass. "I tell you," cried Arne, pulling at his beard, "we must be like little children again. We must bring back color into the world. That is what color is for, to look at. Do not think: paint. Like children."

He pounded the table, clutched his beard, and roared like a bull. He was perfectly happy. I asked him whether he expected the children to understand his paintings, and he gave me a look of scorn. "Only an artist," he declared, "can hope to understand what another artist is trying to do. That is why there is so little understanding of art among the masses.

"Just the same," he added inconsequentially, "the museums are always full of children."

It was always like that with Arne.

As we went out into the street again after supper, on our way home, he said to me in a hopeful way,

"Is this model of yours coming to the Cape this summer, Eben?"

I answered almost without thinking. "Yes," I said. "Some day." He nodded his great head thoughtfully. "Good," he said. "I shall do a portrait of her, myself."

It amused me, and I laughed quietly in the darkness. That would be something to see, that picture.

But it made me feel lonely all of a sudden. I wondered where Jennie was, and what she was doing — in what far off place over which this velvet blue and soft spring evening of ours had long since passed like a wind. Was she still at sea? Night was on the sea, the dark sweep of earth's shadow; but tomorrow's sun was already rising above the eastern slopes of the Urals. And yesterday's sun? did it still shine on the low stone wall at the meadow's edge, near the little wood? It was still today, still noon on the Pacific, on the long, blue swells which washed Hawaii. Yesterday . . . tomorrow . . . where were they?

It would be a long time until Jennie came back to me. Not until we could be together always, she had said. A long summer . . . Hurry, I said to her, in my heart.

I knew that I could never explain it to Arne. I didn't try.

The damp sea air, salty and fresh from the flats, or suddenly pierced with spice from the flowering gardens of Provincetown, flowed around us as we wandered home under the white street lamps. In the harbor the riding lights of the *Mary P. Goulart* rocked gently in the gloom; the beams of the lighthouses at Long Point and Wood End, blinked at the bay; and the great white cross of High Land Light at North Truro swept like the spokes of a wheel through the heavens. The stars burned calmly overhead . . . how many years ago had those metallic rays first leaped out across the empty spaces between their home and ours? Long, long ago; from beyond our furthest yesterday.

The gulls were sleeping out on the water, in the blue dark, silent and forgetful, ranged in rows along the decks of the empty fishing boats. The streets were quiet and deserted; we heard our footsteps following us home.

CHAPTER 16

But I didn't want to stay in Provincetown for the summer. I still had more than two hundred dollars left of the money I had received for the portrait, and I decided to take a small house in Truro, on the Pamet. It was little more than a shack, really, up on the bluff above the water; the pines stood close, making a brown carpet of needles all around the house, and you looked down at the river through their branches. I could hear the waters of the bay endlessly sounding, and the wind in the pines, not unlike the sound of the sea. The air was warm and sweet with the odor of earth and sun, and there was shelter from the easterly rains, and from the northwest wind, which soared up strong and cold over Cornhill behind me. I was right in the path of a southeast blow, or a smoky sou'wester, but that was an advantage; the winds from the south were fair weather winds, and came in warm and soft.

At low tide the Pamet is no more than a trickle of water among the reeds; but at full moon, and with a full course tide, it overflows the marshes, and one can imagine it as it once was, before the sand piled up at the harbor mouth — a wide, deep river on which as many as thirty whalers could ride to their moorings. But that was long ago. To-day the little river pours in and out of a narrow channel to the bay, and wanders crookedly across the Cape between the bay and the ocean. Perhaps a hundred yards from where the Pamet rises among its springs, the low dunes begin; and just across them is the beach and the sea. It's not a long trip from ocean to bay; the Cape is narrow at that end, less than three miles wide.

The little houses nestle in the hollows, safe from the northwest winds which blow so hard in winter. There is pine, and scrub oak, locust, aspen, and elm, bearberry, gorse, wintergreen, beach plum, and cherry. Everything is on a small scale; the tiny hills and hollows, seen in perspective, have the appearance of mountains and valleys. The spires of the two old churches and the meeting house dominate everything; they rise on the highest ridge, and brood serene and lovely over the valleys.

Families still live in Truro from the old days: the Snows, the Dyers, the Atwoods, Atkinses, Cobbs, Paines, Riches. Old names, old families of Cape Cod. . . . It is their country, their home, it belongs to them. They are quiet and kind, hard-working people.

I settled down to work, too. But for a week or so, the colors of the Cape made all my senses drowsy — the pale sand-yellow, the light green, and the faded blue of water and sky deepening off to violet in the distance. Birds on their way north were stopping off to visit; robins searched the lawns, finches darted like minnows in and out of the trees, a pair of orioles had built a nest in the elm tree back of my house.

By June the gorse was yellow, and the bear-berries pink and white on the downs; bob-whites called to each other in the grass. I went down to swim in the river; it was swift and fresh, and the little green crabs fled away from me in the shallows. Some children were there already, playing in an old hulk drawn up on the shore. One, with hair the color of hay, was playing that he was a pirate. He had his crew ready for battle; they consisted of a cap pistol, and his sister. He could not find an enemy.

All summer the children play on the beaches. They are happy and friendly; as each wave sweeps in across the sand, the smaller ones turn their backs to the sea, and run sensibly away. When the water, edged with foam, draws back again, they go running after it, with an air of driving the ocean before them. But at the next wave, they flee as before, with shrill alarm, and fresh surprise. The sun warms their small brown legs, and they collect with enthusiasm bits of clam shell, sand dollars, and colored stones worn by the tide. The larger children plunge into the waves like little dolphins. The water is clear and cold.

Time stands still in Truro; the weeks slip by, one after another. In June there was a nor'easter, the wind came whistling in from the sea, driving the rain almost level before it; it blew for three days, doors swelled and stuck, bureau drawers wouldn't open, and a green mold appeared on some of my canvases. Even the pine logs which burned all day in the fireplace couldn't keep my little house warm or dry. Then the wind swung around to the west, the sun came out, and there was the summer again, the pale sand-yellow, the light green, and the faded blue.

I did a good deal of painting: I did a canvas of the South Truro church for Miss Spinney, the old building, lonely and empty on the downs above the bay; and a watercolor of the sea from the end of Long Nook valley. It was a breezy day, with the wind northeast, the sea was dark, the wine-dark of the Greeks, with bands of green in it, darkening out to the horizon; and the sky was like the inside of a blue porcelain bowl with the light shining through it. I sent them both to Mr. Mathews. But the best thing I did was a painting of the men out in the traps in the early morning. I had to do it mostly from memory: the boats go out to the nets before it's light.

Everything is quiet and dark, the water comes in in long swells out of the darkness. The boats head out into the swells . . . in the east the sky turns grey, and then pink, the dawn comes up slowly. The stars pale out, tones of blue begin to show in the sky. Far out from shore, one boat slips into the traps, drawing the nets up as it goes. The fish are down there, they pass backwards and forwards under the boat like shadows. The nets come higher; suddenly they break water in a rush of silver, and the fishermen begin scooping them in over the sides. The sun rises, the bay sparkles in the light, the fish are silver underfoot. Slowly and heavily one of the boats crosses the bay to Provincetown, while the other heads back again to the shore.

I wanted Arne to go with me, but he said there wasn't enough color in it for him. He was painting the Provincetown Electric Light and Power Plant; he said that it represented industry, and that industry represented the real world of today, and that it was this real world in which an artist should look for a subject worthy of him.

"Let us not fool ourselves, Eben," he exclaimed. "Beauty is only noble when it is useful. The symbol of the world today is a power plant; and if it appears ugly to us, that is only because we do not look at it in the right way."

But he came to Truro for the beach picnics in July. We lay on the sand at Cornhill, while the sun set, and the moon rose over the hill behind us, and men in corduroys and women with kerchiefs around their hair tended the fire of driftwood gathered on the beach. The sunset paled away into rose and green; the old blue night came down dim and hazy over the shore, and across the bay the lanterns of Provincetown twinkled in the dusk. Within the leaping yellow light of our fire the figures of our friends moved about; more wood was gathered, baskets unpacked, rugs laid down. As the flames burned lower toward the coals, steaks and sausages were broiled; a great bean pot was set beside the fire, a pail of mussels, a kettle of coffee. Afterwards we sang, sitting around the fire, while the moon sailed gently overhead, and the tide sent little ripples to break against the sand . . . "*I dream of Jeannie with the light brown hair . . .*"

Or in the still, warm afternoons of August, we swam together in the sea, as the long rollers came lifting in, green and clear, to break in a bounce of foam, and slide hissing and dying up the beach. Far out, beyond the line of the horizon, beyond sight, over the world's rim, lay Europe, torn with her wars; but here all was peace, the empty shore curved away endlessly to the south under the summer sun, the light breeze stirred the grasses on the dunes, and only the shouts of children rose against the rolling thunder of the sea.

It was then that I longed for Jennie, at such times as these, when the world's beauty fell most upon my heart. And yet, in a way which I found hard to explain, I was not lonely; for I had a sense — as I have had ever since — of not being alone — a feeling that the world and Jennie and I were one, joined together in a unity for which there was no name, an inexpressible one-ness. Her very absence, not only from my sight, but from the slow-wheeling days around me, made them seem less real and solid to me; she was nowhere in the weather, the rains which fell across the Cape were not the rains which fell upon her little figure hurrying along somewhere — in what city, in what year? — yet for that reason all weathers seemed one weather to me, and the seasons of the past mingled in my dreams with the summer all around me. For she was somewhere in the world; and wherever she was, there, too, was something of me.

She had said: "How beautiful the world is, Eben. It was never made for anything but beauty — whether we lived now, or long ago."

We had that beauty together. We never lost it.

CHAPTER 17

SUMMER drained away into fall, but Jennie did not return. By September the bearberries were red, and people were picking beach plums in the fields along the roads, to make into jelly. The reeds in the river were silver-brown; and in the afternoons the sun slanted lower through the pines around my house. The birds which had been gone most of the summer, began to appear again, on their way south: red-headed woodpeckers, bluebirds, warblers, and grackles. Swallows swept nervously through the air, and sometimes at evening I saw a wedge of wild duck wavering southward against the sky.

I had received a good-sized check from Mr. Mathews, and decided to use some of it to rent a little sailboat from John Worthington's brother, Bill, who lived near the railroad bridge, close to where the Pamet emptied into the bay. I knew something about sailing, though not a great deal; but I didn't think I could get into much trouble. The boat, an eighteen-foot center-board knock-about, was kept moored near the mouth of the river, in a small backwater to one side of the swiftly moving stream. It took a good bit of navigating to get out into the bay, through the narrow channel; tide and wind both had to be right, but the wind seemed almost always easterly that month, streaming back from the Bermuda high which stood like a formidable but invisible cloud somewhere out at sea; and with a stiff breeze behind me, I could usually manage to make out, even against the tide. Coming back, I had to wait for the current, and then come in close-hauled. Arne constituted himself my crew; he sat forward, ducked the boom when we came about, and handled the jib sheets with a sort of wild solemnity. It was exciting to lean against the wind, and feel the boat fight back against it; to watch the green water slide by, and hear the current chuckle against the planking. It was good exercise, too; it made my arms ache, and put blisters on my hands.

We used to sail out into the bay, sometimes as far as the traps, once or twice as far as Provincetown. It was a world by itself, out there on the water, in the shine and sun-dazzle, a world of never-ending blue, of steady wind, of clear and arrowy distance; and I was happy there.

Late in September a hurricane was reported in the Caribbean. We thought little about it, it was the time of year for hurricanes, they either hit the Florida Keys, or blew themselves out in the Atlantic. This one apparently was headed for Florida.

On the Cape we had a period of unusually clear weather — a weather-breeder, Arne said. We made the most of it, for the season was drawing to an end, the line storm would be along soon, and after that it would be too cold and rough for sailing. We went out every day. The weather was warm — unnaturally so for that time of year — and the wind southeast. We waited for it to swing around into the north.

On Monday the report was that the storm had missed Florida, and was heading for the Carolinas. That meant rain and a southwest blow; but on Tuesday we heard that it had turned east again, and would lose itself out at sea. So we figured we still had a few days' good sailing weather left to us, and decided to make a long trip up the coast, camp over night on Great Island off Wellfleet, and come home the next day. We left a little before noon on Tuesday; there was a steady breeze from the southeast, and we made a fair reach of it all the way.

We camped that night on the island, and built a fire at the sand's edge. We talked for a long time in the firelight; the shadows danced in the scrub behind us, the pale sky, sown with its stars, lay like a great lake above us, and the little boat rocked quietly at its anchor, on the tide. I tried to tell Arne something of what was in my mind, about myself, and about the world. "We know so little," I said, "and there's so much to know. We live by taste and touch; we see only what is under our noses. There are solar systems up there above us, greater than our own; and whole universes in a drop of water. And time stretches out endlessly on every side. This earth, this ocean, this little moment of living, has no meaning by itself . . . Yesterday is just as true as today; only we forget."

Arne yawned. "Yes," he said. "So it is. Go to sleep."

"And love," I said, "is endless, too; and today's little happiness is only part of it."

"Go to sleep," said Arne. "Tomorrow is another day."

That night, for the first time in my life, I dreamed of Jennie: I dreamed of our meeting, long ago, I dreamed it over again as it had happened; I saw her as the child, walking down the long empty row of benches in the Mall, and I heard her say as she had said then, "I wish you'd wait for me to grow up, but you won't, I guess." And in my dream, I remembered the words of her little tuneless song —

"The wind blows, the sea flows . . ."

I woke with a sense of alarm, with a feeling that something was wrong. The wind was still blowing, warm and steadily southeast, but I thought a little stronger. There was a faint haze in the air, and a few strange looking clouds passed by overhead. They seemed to be travelling fast. I leaned over and shook Arne by the shoulder. " Get up, Arne," I said. " We've got to get home."

We put the sail up and headed north for Truro. We didn't waste any time. Out on the water, the wind seemed even stronger; it was a little aft of us, and I let the sail take all it would. It was something of a job to hold the tiller, for a fair sea was running, and the boat yawed a good deal. Arne said nothing; he kept watching the sky.

The haze deepened very slowly, but the clouds increased; they were at different levels, moving rapidly, and of a shape I'd never seen before — long cylinders, fog-like tentacles, smoky fingers. They were a different tone of white, too, like cotton gone a little dusty. I had made the main sheet fast, but I wondered if the sail would hold. " Arne," I called to him, " hadn't we better reef? "

He nodded without speaking, and I managed

to bring the boat up into the wind. I noticed that my fingers were trembling, and I thought that Arne looked a little pale. There was a curious urgency in the wind. "We'd better get out of here," I said.

The boat went off with a rush under a single reef, and I tried to head up a little to windward, to get some shelter from the shore. The waves were running a good deal higher now, and breaking at the crests; I had to put all my weight on the tiller to hold her steady. I was feeling decidedly uneasy, and I wondered whether I oughtn't to try to make for shore directly, but there was nowhere except the Pamet at Truro where I could have found shelter for the boat. I had no idea how hard the wind was blowing, but I knew it was blowing hard. And there was a strange sound to it, from somewhere far away.

A little before noon I saw Arne point behind us, and followed his glance back over the stern. The horizon to the south had disappeared behind a grey haze. It wasn't altogether grey, but grey-yellow, like mud. I thought perhaps it was rain, but it didn't look like it. We've got to get out of this, I thought.

My arms and hands were aching from holding the tiller, and my legs were tired from bracing my-self against the sides. I beckoned Arne to come aft and take over, while I went forward to bail some of the water that had come in, mostly over the stern. Down in the cockpit, the waves seemed higher than ever; we would tilt up at the stern, hang for a moment on a crest, and then rush down the slope after it, and slew around in the hollow till Arne straightened us out. Each time the tip of the boom hit the water, I thought we'd go over. My throat was dry, but I didn't feel frightened, I didn't have time. I kept listening to the wind; it wasn't like anything I'd ever heard before.

A little after that we started to work in toward the Pamet. I went back to the tiller, and told Arne to take the sheet, and let it out whenever we got over too far. He snubbed it around a cleat as well as he could, but it took all his great strength to hold it. We lay out to windward on the deck, with our legs braced against the centerboard scabbard; the huge seas broke behind us, and then foamed up over the counter, and the dark green water poured along the leeward deck up to the coaming. It seemed to me that we looked right down at the sea under our feet; it rose sometimes in a slice of wave and curled up over the cockpit; then I kicked the tiller, and we came up. We seemed half in and half out of the water most of the time, I couldn't tell which. "I think we'll make it, though," I said. Arne shook his head. "Maybe," he answered.

About two hundred yards from shore, the mainsail went out, torn loose near the peak; and a moment later, the jib. I thought we were done for then; but both sails caught in the rigging and snagged, and the boat eased. I saw that as long as they held, we had a sort of double reef; and we hadn't much further to go. " I think we'll make it, Arne," I said.

I could barely see the river mouth for the waves, which gave me an idea of how high the tide was running; but I set a course for the railroad bridge, and trusted to luck. We hit it right, and went in through a white fury of foam, on a roaring breaker which picked us up and ran us up the channel like a chip of wood, and flung us out on the sand a hundred yards from the bay. Arne was out first, but before he could get the mainsail down, the wind tore it out of his hands, and sent it ballooning across the river, with half the rigging attached to it. We got the anchor out, but I knew it wouldn't hold. The waves were booming in through the river mouth, six feet high, and coming up the channel like wild horses. " It's no good, Arne," I said. " The tide's coming in; she'll drag right down to the bridge, and lose her mast." There was nothing we could do. I hadn't figured on such a high tide.

Bill Worthington had seen us come in. He was waiting for us as we climbed up onto the road from what was left of the beach. "Well, by God," he said, "you boys were out in something."

I grinned back at him, but I felt pretty shaky. My legs were trembling, and I couldn't keep my teeth together. "I'm sorry about the boat, Bill," I said. "I didn't figure the storm would be so bad."

Bill looked at me, and shook his head. "Storm, hell," he said. "This one's a hurricane."

CHAPTER 18

BILL told us that hurricane signals were flying at High Land Light; he said it made him feel queer in the pit of his stomach. But it was still only the beginning; we all knew that.

We made the boat fast as well as we could, and then Bill drove us home to the north side of the river. We could hear the sand pit against the car whenever we crossed an exposed place in the road, and once or twice the car swerved sharply in a sudden gust. Bill left us at the house, and went back to watch the tide. His own house wasn't any too far above high water.

It was only then, as we started down the path to the shack, that I began to have an idea of what the wind was really like. Out there, on the water, I'd been too busy; and besides, in a sort of way, we had been part of it, moving with it, running before it. But here, facing the open sweep from the southeast, I caught it full and fair, and it hit me like a blow.

The wind was coming across the Pamet in a steady flow, almost like a river of air in flood. There was no let up to it, it came flowing over heavy and solid and fast; it had pushed the marsh grass down flat, and bent the pines over in a quarter circle. There was something unnatural about it; it seemed to be coming from far away, but all the time it was coming nearer, and I had a feeling that it was darkness itself coming, and a force that didn't belong on this earth. My heart was beating fast; I felt cold and excited. I could hear that strange sound I had heard out on the bay, a sort of roaring hum, high up and far off; and the yellow-gray wall was still down there to the south. Or had it come closer? I couldn't tell. I looked down the slope at the river; it was up over the marsh, and the water was brown, and streaked with yellow foam. "I'm glad we're here," I said to Arne, shouting against the wind. He smiled then, for the first time. "If the house holds," he said.

A branch from a locust down at the water's edge suddenly snapped, and sailed a few yards up the slope toward us. "Come on," I said; "let's go in."

We went around the back way, to get out of the direct force of the wind. While we'd been gone the grocer had left a box of eggs on the little back porch; they were all over the floor. I thought, that'll be a mess to clean up tomorrow, but I didn't stop. The wind picked us up, and swept us in through the door, and we had to lean back against it to close it. It was cold and still in the house, but I could hear the roaring in my ears, from those hours out on the bay. After a while the noise in my ears went away, and then I could hear the storm itself, and that high, far off, humming sound.

Arne made a fire, and I got out the whiskey. I took a big drink; I could feel it warm me all the way down. We stood in front of the fire, and looked at each other. I could feel the house shake every now and then, and I heard the windows rattle; I wondered if I ought to try to put up the shutters, I tried to remember what I'd read about hurricanes. But then I remembered that the house had no shutters. There didn't seem to be anything to do.

"I wonder if the boat will hold," I said.

"I wouldn't think so," said Arne.

"We were lucky, at that," I said.

I took another drink. "I wonder how they're making out in Provincetown," I said.

Arne shook his head gloomily. "It'll be bad, all right," he remarked.

The rain began about then. It wasn't much of a downpour, but it came in almost level. In ten minutes there was a fair-sized puddle just inside the door. I laid a towel along the lintel, to keep the water out.

The wind seemed to be getting stronger all the time; once or twice it shook the house so hard I thought the walls would go. There was nothing to do but just sit there and wait for something to happen; and after a while, Arne said he thought we ought to go out and have a look around. He said he wanted to see what a hurricane looked like. We went out the back way, and it took all our strength to get the door closed after us. But when we got around to the front of the house, we couldn't breathe; the wind tore the air right out of our mouths. "Boy," said Arne, holding his hands in front of his face, "I'm glad I'm not out on the bay now."

I tried to see the bay, but it was lost in weather, a gray smother of rain and spray and blowing sand. I saw that the telegraph poles beyond Cat Island were down, and I pointed at them. And then the big elm behind the house went.

It went over slowly, with a sort of sigh, taking a lot of ground with it. Arne didn't say anything, but his eyes had a wild look in them. He grabbed my arm, and pointed across the river. A moment later we saw Bill Worthington's old barn sag over on its side, and watched the wind worry it along toward the river. "Maybe we ought to go over and help him," I shouted, with my mouth close to Arne's ear. He made a gesture of helplessness. "How are we going to get there?" he shouted back.

We were still watching Bill's house, crouched together with our arms wrapped around one of the straining pines, when the coastguard truck came by. It stopped on the road behind us, and a guardsman came clumping over in boots and oilskins. "Jeez," he said, "what do you guys think you're doing?" We told him that we were watching Bill's barn being blown into the river. "Well," he said, "there'll be more than that in the river soon. The ocean's breaking through at Dune Hollow." He walked back to the truck, and they went on, toward Cat Island, and John Rule's house out at the edge of the marsh.

We were pretty high above the water where we were, and I didn't think even the ocean would reach that far. At any rate, we didn't have long to wait; in about ten minutes we saw the wave coming down the valley toward us, from the sea. It didn't look very high — just a line of brown foam, with branches and sand in it, but it was scary. It passed under us, and then there wasn't any marsh left, just water, moving fast.

And a moment later, I saw her.

She was below me, and a little to the east, near the town landing, trying to get up the slope from the river. She seemed tired; and the wind was worrying her like a dog. While I watched, she lost her balance, and half fell; and then she began to slip backward toward the water again. Another wave was coming down the valley from the east; I could see it coming.

I don't know how I got down the hill to her, against the wind, but I did. I got my arm around her just in time, and pulled her up out of the way; the crest went by almost a foot below us. She lay back against me, white and spent, with closed eyes. "I was afraid I wouldn't get here, darling," she said.

I held her close. Even then, with that mad flood below us, I thought we'd make it all right. I put my face down against hers; her cheeks were deathly cold. She lifted her hands slowly, as though they were a great weight, and put her arms around my neck. "I had to get back to you, Eben," she said.

"We'll have to hurry, Jennie," I told her. I tried to pull her along, up the slope, but she was like a dead weight, she seemed to have no strength left at all. She smiled at me piteously, and shook her head. "You go, Eben," she said; "I can't make it."

I tried to lift her, then, but she was too heavy for me; I couldn't find a foothold on the slippery ground. The water was higher, now, almost at our feet; a dark ripple washed in over my ankles. "Jennie," I cried, "for God's sake . . ."

"Let me look at you," she whispered. I couldn't hear her, but I knew what she was saying. She held my face in her hands, and looked at me for a moment with wide, dark eyes. "It's been a long time, darling," she said.

I didn't want to talk, I wanted to get out of there, I wanted to get her up the slope away from the water. "Look," I said, "if I could lift you up on my back . . ."

But she didn't seem to hear me. "Yes," she said, almost to herself; "I wasn't wrong."

"Jennie," I cried; "please . . ."

Her arms tightened around me for a moment. "Hold me close, Eben," she said. "We're together, now."

I held her close, but my mind was in a panic. I couldn't lift her, I couldn't get her away, and the ground where we were standing was beginning to give. "Arne," I shouted as loudly as I could; "Arne."

It was then I saw it coming.

It came in from the bay, a great brown wave, sweeping back up the valley toward the sea. There was no escape from it; we could never have climbed above it; it came in steady and very fast, with a strange sucking noise. Well, I thought, we'll go together, anyhow.

Bending over, I kissed her full on the lips. "Yes, Jennie," I said; "we're together now."

She knew what was coming. "Eben," she whispered, pressed against my cheek, "there's only one love . . . nothing can change it. It's still all right, darling, whatever happens, because we'll always be together . . . somewhere . . ."

"I know," I said.

And then the wave hit us. I tried to hold on to her, to go out with her, but it tore us apart. I felt her whirled out of my arms; the water drew me under, and rolled me over and over; I felt myself flung upwards, sucked down, and then flung upwards again. Then something crashed into me, and that was all I knew.

Arne found me sprawled in a tree half in and half out of the water, and dragged me back to safety. How he managed to carry me up the slope and back to the house in that wind, I don't know. He put me to bed, and made me drink almost a pint of whiskey; and he sat beside me all that night. He told me later that he had to hold me down in bed, that I kept trying to get back to the river. I don't remember much about it, it was all dark for me, all I remember is the dark.

It was a week before I could travel, but it made no difference, because the roads were out, and we couldn't have gotten through, anyway. I lay in bed, and ate what Arne gave me, and tried not to think about what had happened. Arne brought back the news from outside; he told me that there hadn't been as much damage in Truro as we'd thought; a lot of trees had gone over in Provincetown, and a fishing boat had been flung up on the rocks; John Worthington's nets were gone at North Truro, but except for the ocean breaking through into the Pamet, it hadn't been so bad. Even Bill's home had escaped, though the water had come up as high as the windows. The beach at Dune Hollow had started to build up again; pretty soon everything would be the same as before.

I came back to the city on a bright autumn day, deep blue and sun-yellow in the streets, and the great buildings rising clear and sharp in the keen, high air. Mr. Mathews was waiting for me at the gallery. "We worried about you, Eben," he said. "Miss Spinney and I . . . we couldn't get any news for a long while."

He patted me awkwardly on the shoulder. "I'm glad to see you, my boy," he said. "I — I'm very glad . . ."

Miss Spinney didn't say anything. She looked to me as though she had been crying.

It was Gus who gave me the little clipping from the newspaper. "I thought maybe you hadn't seen it, Mack," he said.

It was from the Times, of September 22nd.

" The steamship Latania," it read, " has reported by wireless today the loss of one of its passengers in the storm, a hundred miles off the Nantucket Lightship. Miss Jennie Appleton, who was returning to America after a stay of eight years abroad, was swept overboard by a wave which smashed a part of the bridge, and injured several of the passengers. Officials of the line are endeavoring to discover the whereabouts of Miss Appleton's relatives in this country."

Gus hesitated; he looked at me, and then he looked away. " I thought maybe you didn't know," he said. " I'm sorry, Mack."

I gave the clipping back to him. " No," I said, " I knew.

" It's still all right," I said. " It's all right."

Truro,
1949

A NOTE ON THE TYPE

This book is set in Linotype Caledonia. Caledonia belongs to the family of printing types called "modern face" by printers — a term used to mark the change in style of type-letters that occurred about 1800. Caledonia is in the general neighborhood of Scotch Modern in design, but is more freely drawn than that letter.

The book was designed by W. A. Dwiggins, and composed, printed, and bound by The Plimpton Press, Norwood, Massachusetts. The paper was made by S. D. Warren Company, Boston.